p.s.

The Revisionist
Out of Time
Not a Free Show
Wanting a Child (Coedited with Jill Bialosky)

p.s.

A NOVEL

HELEN SCHULMAN

BLOOMSBURY

Copyright © 2001 by Helen Schulman

Published by Bloomsbury, New York and London.

Distributed to the trade by St. Martin's Press.

Library of Congress Cataloging-in-Publication Data

Schulman, Helen.
P.S. / by Helen Schulman.
p. cm.
ISBN 1-58234-157-5 (alk. paper)
1. Middle aged women – Fiction. 2. Divorced women – Fiction. I. Title

PS3569.C5385 P18 2001
813'54--dc21
00-067472

First Edition

10 9 8 7 6 5 4 3 2 1

Typeset by Palimpsest Book Production Limited,
Polmont, Stirlingshire

Printed and bound in the United States of America
by R. R. Donnelley & Sons Company, Crawfordsville

Bruce!

Zoë!

Isaac!

For their general support and strange faith, the author
would like to thank: Sloan Harris, Karen Rinaldi,
Elizabeth Gaffney, my parents, Elissa Schappel,
Dani Shapiro, Ilena Silverman and the folks at *GQ*,
Joan Aguado, Philomen Lancaster, Bruce Handy,
and always
Charlie Schulman, brother extraordinaire.

It had been a long time between drinks of water for Louise Harrington. There was an early summer lurking outside her office window, and if she craned her neck between the stacks of applications and the piles of folders that rose above her windowsill – like a miniature skyline – she could see that beyond her little office the world was full of boys.

Shaggy boys with bandannas leapt through the air like golden retrievers to catch Frisbees with the open jaws of their palms. There were boys without shirts on. Boys banging on bongos and blowing harmonicas and playing guitar; boys hunched over on the lawn, their shoulder blades cutting sharp and provocative angles through their torn, stained T-shirts, their heartfelt utterances – those whiny lyrics – setting off a beating of their wings. Boys singing badly. There were boys lounging, on the cement, on the grass, their heads pillowed by balled-up sweatshirts and backpacks and jean jackets; boys soaking up the sun. There were boys wading in the fountains, jeans cuffed past their hairy calves, and boys already in this warm breeze venturing outside in cutoff shorts. There were boys sleeping, and boys smoking and reading Nietzsche and Derrida and *On The Road,* boys kicked back and listening to tunes on headsets and boom boxes and grooving to space jams in their minds; there were boys bent over coffee and boys tipping back beers and even one boy drinking milk out of the carton like he was standing in front of an open refrigerator in Mom's kitchen back home. There were boys making the moves. Staring – directly into some lucky someone's eyes. There were hundreds of boys, it seemed, leaning into hundreds of lank skinny girls, in lank skinny skirts; all these young, newly hatched, still downy couples hanging out on the great grand limestone steps of the central library of Columbia University. They were half Louise's age. They looked like they were getting plenty. What had happened to her life?

Louise turned to the application in her lap. This particular candidate wanted to be a sculptor, he wanted to be a Master of Fine Arts, and he wanted this divine transformation to occur at the very fine institution where just yesterday she had been appointed the acting admissions coordinator. He had been born in 1979. He was graduating early from Bennington College and he liked to work with metal. He liked to weld. Louise's bony, ringless fingers fluttered over his three recommendation letters, lingering on his personal essay which went on, quite grandiosely, about the majesty of the Twin Towers, which was why, he wrote, 'the spiritual essences of these architectural giants have been transported into my brain where they have taken over and acted as my "muse".'

Transported? Into his brain? Was he a bad writer, or was he a paranoid-schizophrenic? She fanned through the rest of his package: three recommendation letters (which no one would pay attention to, unless the recommender said that the kid was a psycho, or the letter itself was written by the Pope, or Richard Serra), a series of slides, his dubious undergraduate records, a statement of intent. With a check made out to the university for seventy-five dollars his application was complete, so Louise transferred it into a green complete-application folder, color-coded the exterior with three circular stickers (red, yellow, blue; Louise loved the purity of primary colors), and set it aside for the first of his corresponding three readers, the harried adjunct associate professors who made up the bulk of the Fine Arts faculty. If experience proved anything, this folder would make its way back to Louise in record time, an academic boomerang, dotted with spilled sips of coffee, a splash of ramen noodles, the dark inky fingerprints of criminals being booked and readers of the *New York Times*, the sloppy proof that the application had been perused. But this Bennington boy's review would likely be cursory at best. Perhaps, while an instructor was en route to Columbia from The New School, scrambling to teach her eighth class of the week, the slides would be held up for critique under the advancing lights of a northbound subway.

Louise looked out the window again. She looked at all those young unfettered students, doing their thing, making their way, making out. Who could blame her for her choices?

She'd gotten married. She'd gotten married too young to someone too old. That must have been it. That must have been why so much had gone wrong in what once had seemed so practically perfect. Not that Peter was literally old back then; he wasn't literally old now, really; it wasn't like Louise had run off with a widower with grown children or anything, with an ageing macher with a big belly, a fat wallet, important friends, and a good car, who on weekends liked to listen to classical music and lie on the couch; she hadn't married her father for heaven's sake. *Thank God,* her mother's voice rang inside her head. Instead, she had married her astronomy professor. And she'd divorced him, four years ago, after ten years of marriage, which was how, she figured, she happened to end up exactly where she was right now.

She got up, stretched, leaned out her open window. Were any of the kids down below aware of her, still attractive she surmised, and in damn good aerobic shape, Louise noted with pride, full of yearning and desire and need? Did any of them give a shit really, that Louise was toiling away upstairs, in a prestigious newly elevated position, sure, but honestly for peanuts, truly for their benefit; looking out for their future resumés and biographies and careers? Selfish boys, selfish girls. Why weren't they aware of her, locked up like Rapunzel in her tower, laboring away on their behalf? Didn't any of them bother to think when they brushed past her in a stairwell, that the woman they dared to call 'Ma'am' when excusing their own clumsy behavior, had once been an exalted version of one of their own? The kind of coed who had managed to run off with her instructor.

Peter Harrington, her now ex-husband, was still kind and still smart and still good. His handsomeness had become more shovellike as the years had passed; his face had broadened and grown appropriately lined; he still had wide shoulders and small hips, although now his belly jutted out a little past his belt. He was steady and reliable; careerwise he'd attained a formidable gravitas. He was not a rogue, nor a loose cannon, Peter. And he was still her best friend – *pretty much your only friend,* her mother's voice rang inside her head again – and he still taught physics at this same university where Louise presently worked discovering artists – sifting through applications like a gold prospector, searching for those infinitesimally small nuggets of talent – and lusting in her heart after mere children. Often, she and Peter would have dinner; she'd order in for him or he would cook for her, they would stay up talking late in either one of their university-subsidized apartments, and as the evening waxed on maybe one or the other would begin wondering sleepily about what had gone wrong between them. But never had one of those evenings slipped them out of their clothes and into a bed. And although she had dated some right after their divorce, and if truth be told, also a little prior to it, it had been a while since Louise had fucked anybody.

At the moment, outside her office, the air was so fragrant with cherry blossoms and freshly mown grass and mud and the spicy thick scent of marijuana, that each passing breeze drove Louise crazy, making her legs cross and her teeth itch. Her new office, computer-colored and square, had been decorated by her tasteful predecessor with ivy-filled mossy hanging baskets, lovely groupings of old chipped china – tea sets, squat little vintage tin kettles, some graceful cups and saucers, one or two especially handsome plates on stands – on the walls hung antique prints of apples, pears, ferns, everything a lacy green and white. It wasn't exactly to

Louise's taste – she would have preferred something more austere – but that very morning it had seemed just pleasant enough to float her through the academic term; it would do. By afternoon, however, the breeze had whipped all that greenery into a hothouse frenzy, and Louise understood why her predecessor had run screaming out of this room on just such a lovely day last week, vowing never to return. A loyal, conscientious employee, this woman had spent the previous Thursday and Friday training Louise over the phone; she said she was moving to the rolling hills of Virginia, where she'd open up a store of curios and tchotchkes and antiques, and live finally like a person. Louise had had far too many administrative questions to ask, so she hadn't gotten around to the most obvious and most salient: How *does* one live like a person? And why, exactly, would one want to?

Now the oily and complex musk of garbage and pushcart shish kebabs and exhaust that usually characterized upper Broadway barely hinted underneath the skirts of this fecund spring perfume. Louise put the stack of applications on the floor, stood and leaned over towards the window to breathe in heavily, then raised her arms so that the wind would pass through her simple linen sheath, a pale and attractive yellow, bought at Barney's during a weak moment, when Louise had dared herself to do anything at all, no matter how reckless or foolish or vain or ultimately inconsequential it was, in order to somehow change her life. Peter had teased, she remembered now, a little cruelly, she'd thought, when she'd worn that stupid, smart, elegant dress to a lunch they'd had ad hoc, a few weeks prior, between classes, on the library steps, when she'd eaten her pizza over the marble, holding the slice away from her body, away from that sumptuous fabric. 'What a waste of an entire post-tax week's salary,' Peter had laughed, dabbing at his mouth with a linen hankie Louise had bought for him as a gift on their last anniversary, a day they didn't necessarily celebrate any more since their divorce, but a day she could hardly forget either, and then, to add insult to injury, Peter had said: 'Who are you dressing for, anyway, the work-study students?' *Oh, you must have asked for it* – there was Mom's voice in her head again, clamorous and insistent – *Peter must have been having a bad day, a terrible day, to speak that way to anyone, you must have done something to provoke him, Louise, or perhaps you misread his tone, Peter would never speak that way to you, Peter wouldn't speak that way to a dogcatcher.* A dogcatcher? Were there still dogcatchers left on the planet? There are dream catchers, Mom, thought Louise, there are celebrity journalists, and fashion editors and the pathological liars who churn out pop songs, there are baseball catchers and Catchers in the Rye and cootie catchers, maybe Peter was a cootie-catcher, Mom, maybe he was one of those little fucker athletes in grade school who kept catching cooties off of all those academic achievers, who didn't know whether it was better in the long run to laugh or cry when they were being accosted, inevitably losing either way. Louise tried to picture Peter chasing after some pale-skinned, highwater-wearing A-student in the grade school playground, but for the life of her she couldn't. He'd been an A-student himself, and an athlete; he'd been all-American in high school track, a ringer in Little League; he'd won the statewide science prize in sixth grade and then again in ninth, a Westinghouse scholarship upon graduation; he'd been a peer counselor, a member of the elementary school student council, he'd been a sensitive little bugger. Peter hadn't had the time, what with all his extracurricular activities, or for that matter, the desire, considering his considerable popularity – he'd been named most beautiful in-and-out in his high school yearbook – or frankly the wherewithal, for his head was always confidently in the clouds, to have spent a moment chasing after anyone. So maybe Mom was right, perhaps Peter was having a particularly lousy day, the day that he was so mean to Louise, the woman he'd once been married to, the woman he'd often claimed to love. Louise hoped Peter's day had positively sucked, for hadn't he ruined hers with his offhand comments, and the possibility of this proving itself true, Peter's day sucking, didn't feel so very farfetched, for Louise guessed with the certainty of a champion that Peter wasn't getting laid any more in the moment than she was. There was pleasure in this vengeful thought. Schadenfreude. She wasn't proud of it, but then again, she wasn't exactly ashamed of it either.

At the open window of her little office she breathed in the cool, spicy breeze along with this pleasure, allowing it to blow right through her exposed neckline, across her underarms, where she was damp. She wore no undergarments, never had, and at thirty-eight doubted she ever would. I'm dressing for myself, thought Louise, God damn it. Using the heels of her hands, Louise slammed that window down.

She had work to do. Rolling admissions. She pivoted towards her desk – wilted paperwhites after a week without water browning like the pages of a rare book, their delicate heads bent at the shoulders, dripping petals upon a letter box made of cracked Delft plate – and as she turned knocked over a pile of folders with a roughened elbow, an elbow that years ago Peter used to massage with cream, after her bath. The folders dominoed to the floor, spilling all those forms covered with sloppy pen and ink that had explicitly stated in bold print: TO BE TYPED, ONLY. The floor was a mess. She fought back the urge to weep.

She fought and fought, that is she only fought once, and then Louise gave in, sobbing without water, the ocular equivalent of dry heaves.

After awhile of this, feeling stupid, ridiculous, *a certified nincompoop* – Mom! – she leaned over, started straightening up. Warshofsky, Evans, Aguado, she'd realphabetize all of them, all the aspiring artists and artistas, their hopes high and soaring, their young hearts pathetically full. When the day was done, when school was over, the lucky ones would often end up working at a gallery somewhere, drinking espresso all day outfitted in Miguel Aldrover. (Wouldn't that be a perfect life for Louise? She made a mental note to pursue it.) The unlucky ones tended bar or taught art in the public schools. Once in a while a genius – or a financial genius! it was rumoured that one of their graduates was Jeff Koons under another name, although he categorically denied it – would emerge from one class or another, which was why, she guessed, these applications kept pouring in, throughout the fall, spring and summer. Winter was the busy season. All that ice and snow, the extra ten pounds, existential doubt. Restlessness.

Aguado, Evans, Warshofsky. Now in proper order. Louise

was accomplishing something. She was working. She picked up another folder. Feinstadt, Scott.

For a moment, her heart stopped. It did that now and again, a little mitral valve prolapse action, a familiar suspension of her most vital organ, like a dancer's leap, she and her life supports hanging in the air, bridging two moments in time. Then came the crash in her chest, the heavy beating of a desperate bird's wings, the poor thing (her heart) banging up against the sliding glass doors of a patio.

Louise caught her breath. Scott Feinstadt. She petted the outside of his folder.

There had been a Scott Feinstadt when she was a girl growing up in Larchmont. Her Scott Feinstadt had been a painter and a printmaker and she'd loved him all her life, for hadn't her life only started then, in high school, that first morning when she'd woken up and thought: I want to know and feel everything! (when now all Louise wanted in the world was to know and feel from nothing). She'd loved him from afar the moment she first saw him, which was registration day freshman year. He had a girlfriend then – Scott Feinstadt always had a girlfriend – a beautiful hippie chick, Roberta Goldman, with long, flowing red-gold hair and ululating Indian skirts and toe rings and earrings and bracelets around her upper arms, one bejeweled job gracing her left ankle. When the two of them, Scott and Berta, as he called her, walked into the school gym arm in arm that morning, the seas parted, and they skipped to the head of the line, directly in front of Louise. Scott's hair was long then, too. It was thick and black with silver gray streaks even in high school, like a smattering of frost had wafted down and graced it; and it was unbrushed and matted in a long, loose ponytail that was tied with a rubber band that Louise could see had only served to tangle and break off his hair. There were many split ends, like a gossamer silver halo around that band.

Three years later, after Berta had been replaced by Trisha the dancer, and Trisha had been replaced by Theresa Longo, the dark-eyed daughter of the proprietor of the lone Italian restaurant in Larchmont, and after Theresa had been dallied with and sent back to the kitchen, he was hers. Scott Feinstadt was hers. He and Louise dated hot and heavy the summer before her senior year. Scott had just returned home from several months in Italy – his parents and his grandmother had refused to continue wiring him advances on his inheritance – so he had come back from Europe to work off his coming art-school expenses in a new food emporium called Cheese Bazaar. It was there that the local mothers first discovered Jarlsberg cheese, quiche and kiwis, pesto sauce and fresh pasta; it was there that, pre-Starbucks, they went for a nice slice of carrot cake and cup of 'fresh ground' coffee. It was at Cheese Bazaar that Louise and her girlfriends escaped the heat, where they went to get their frozen yogurt, after *General Hospital*, after mornings at the Sound squeezing lemon juice on their hair, and on their upper lips and upper thighs, sitting for hours in the sun, reading the thinnest of thin novels and the thickest fashion magazines.

Because she loved Scott Feinstadt from afar while they were in school and while he was away, and then even more acutely when he was back in town toiling at Cheese Bazaar, she often made the trip twice daily. Before and after dinner. Until finally

Scott Feinstadt had been forced to ask her out. She'd wait for him to sweep and close up shop, and then they'd ride around for hours in his beat-up old red truck. He was full of Italian phrases, '*molto bene, grazie bella*', and romantic stories and Louise spent hours listening to him while brushing out his long salt-and-pepper locks, his hair curling wildly and breathing silver fire beneath her hands. They broke up just weeks before he was to drive to Rhode Island to go to art school. 'It's only fair to you,' Scott said, one afternoon in his red truck, after she had given him a blowjob. 'I don't want to hold you back, I want you to have a Wild and Adventurous Life.' Louise. Wild and Adventurous.

It was the drive to Rhode Island that killed him. A highway fatality.

He'd never even gotten to school, never got to test his mettle as an artist, never had time to regret his decision, to come to his senses, go crawling back to Louise, to grovel in the dirt. He'd never even had a chance to miss her.

Nor was she granted the grand prize, the status of being his girlfriend at the time of his death; Scott Feinstadt had started up a little end-of-summer thing with her best friend, Missy, so Louise had none of the dignity of widowhood: Missy, on the other hand, had dined out on it for years.

Still, Louise wept for six months straight, day and night, such a torrent of weeping it seemed to dry her out permanently (she'd not wept since; she'd gulped and cried out during bad periods, but no tear water had slipped down her cheeks); and she'd wandered around the halls of her high school as a thin, ghostly, discoed-out Ophelia – her Fiorucci jeans were held up only by the hanger of her hipbones, her blouses were long and white, gossamer cottons, silky Quianas – so of course all the local boys wanted to take her to the senior prom, go out back into their cars and fuck her. It was her most popular spring and summer, but Louise didn't care then, she cared now!, but she didn't care then. She spurned her lovers one after the other, and even more dramatically, their offers of rides, leaving a trail of ravaged hearts in her wake as she roamed the streets of Larchmont, a lone romantic figure, traversing the little foot path that spanned the commuter rail, on the long walk home from school. Finally, she went to college where no one knew her or cared that she had done a dead boy. Which was a relief. She felt so anonymous, like if she were to fall off the suspension bridge that straddled one of the two icy gorges that bracketed the university, no one would notice until the rapid rush of snow melt uncovered her body during the late, late spring thaw. Until Peter had come along and rescued her.

Louise was still at the tippy-top of her teens back then, the age of most of the boys outside her window, and unlike them, she supposed, she'd been wavery and unformed, as if the staircase of her youth had just landed her on a great, big fluffy cloud bank, and she had had no idea where it was safe to stand. At that moment in her life the last thing she wanted was someone her own age, someone as unanchored and as uncertain as she felt. She hadn't wanted a boy; she'd wanted a man.

He was a knight in shining armor, Peter. Everyone thought so, all her girlfriends, all the gaggle of jealous brainy beauties that swarmed his podium, and of course, Mrs Harrington who had given birth to him. But not her mother. Ellie

Silverstein had spent the first five years of her daughter's marriage trying to talk Louise out of it, and the last five years trying to coax her back inside. How had her own mother carefully tracked the rise and fall of Louise's romantic currency? Practically, with an unwavering intelligence and a keen sense of the odds. 'He's a nice boy,' said Mom, back then, 'for a WASP. But you never even gave yourself a chance.' Now she said: 'You have to give it another chance, Louisey, men like Peter don't grow on trees.'

They didn't, they didn't really. Scott Feinstadt and the boys who came after him, the handful of men that followed the first heady blush of her divorce then trickled off into nothingness, *they* grew on trees. There seemed to be a new crop every generation, all stacked up in the sexy-bad-boyfriend lumberyard. They were smart and selfish and reckless. They looked hot in their paint-splattered torn blue jeans. When they grew up – if they grew up – they grew up to be foreign war correspondents and movie producers and videographers; lazy trust-fund babies and rakish entrepreneurs. These guys were always off somewhere, Bali or Morocco or Bhutan, and they were always hopelessly in love with some Peace Corps gal, or an Iranian photographer, or a gorgeous mixed-race actress who just got cast in an upscale miniseries; some woman who jerked and jerked and jerked them around, who jerked them around so much, they couldn't help jerking you around too, these Scott Feinstadts in their glory. It was the trickle-down theory of romance. As her erstwhile best friend Missy proclaimed: 'Single women are always depositories for relationship runoff.'

They weren't bad, really, these guys, they weren't evil;

they were just too immature or too fucked-up or terminally lovesick. Too damaged. But not Professor Peter Harrington. He was sincere. At the time, Louise thought, looking back with some pleasure, her early marriage had been so out of vogue among her peers – daughters of mothers like her own mother, daughters of women who had denied themselves, married too early, subsumed their own desires and needs to their husbands', their homes, their children; *and then been dumped for some cross-eyed slut!* – that it had been viewed as practically countercultural. It had had its own mysterious élan. But her mother had been on target after all; Louise had married badly and far too young, wasn't that it? Once again, hadn't her mother infuriatingly turned out to be right?

It had been a long time since Louise had been a student, a long time since Peter had been an ambitious junior professor, a genius, maybe, everyone said, the girls in her astronomy section who huddled together in the bathroom during break, gossiping and stealing a smoke, the RA on her floor, a moony physics major with long unwashed blonde hair who held court over air-popped popcorn in the kitchenette back at the dorm. In fact a samizdat underground student publication that served as a crib sheet for course offerings had named Peter 'a superfox with an office', something Louise had clipped out after she'd first laid eyes upon him during orientation, when she was eagerly searching out whatever info she could find on the handsome, personable young prof who had presided over the lectern, without calling too much attention to her own burgeoning curiosity, her crush.

He was a hotshot academic, published and close to tenured, and he was in his late twenties. The difference in their ages,

close to a decade – the same nine-year span that had miraculously shrunk over the years into a statistical insignificance –
provided, at the time, a rather large maturity divide; it was as
if a precocious grade-schooler were going with a high school
guy, an eighth-grader dating a college senior. There was little
Louise Silverstein the art history major, proud to be on the
arm of Peter Harrington, the all-grown-up physics professor.
He taught the section of 'The Universe and You' that she was
enrolled in, the second semester of her sophomore year – a
science requirement she was hoping to get rid of.

Looking out her office window now, somewhat painlessly
glimpsing the tatooed chest of an Ultimate Frisbee player in
midflight, his purple-tressed girlfriend cheering from the side-
lines, Louise remembered the moment Peter finally noticed
her. She'd been looking out the window that long-ago day
too, for a just a second, to the weeping willow outside
her classroom up in Ithaca and then back again, only to
find herself staring straight into the soft brown eyes of her
instructor. How long had he been looking at her like that, so
moist and permeable, so obviously respirating? Peter's eyes
were dilating wounds. Up until that moment, she had thought
of him as 'Professor', something full and strong and smart,
something like 'Doctor', 'President', 'Movie Star'. It surprised
her then that any man of power, of expertise, would conduct
himself this way: his presentation so manifestly human. But
out of the pure biology of his mouth – alive, awash with
saliva, bacteria, outfitted with perfect large white teeth –
came a string of poetry. A sentence Louise instantly knew
was designed to save her. It was the sentence of an angel.
'The calcium in your bones comes from the remnants of dead

stars.' At that moment, Peter's duality, his power and his intensely open desire, both repelled and attracted her, like two refrigerator magnets jockeying in the center of her heart.

Louise had felt herself blush right then, heat and a rising color, and turned her gaze quickly down to the empty page and the dried-up Flair pen that had been lying motionless on her desk for the majority of the semester. She sucked on the end of it, leaving a little blue blot, an inky welling, like a bruise on her bottom lip – a later confession: Peter had noticed that blot! That blot had made his teeth and palms itch! – she picked up that newly moistened marker and drew a blue heart. She was still that young. She was still young enough to be doodling hearts in her margins. And she pretended to be thinking. Profound thoughts in keeping with the tenor of his sentence. But she was dizzy. No man had ever offered himself so nakedly to her before. Could it have been her new perfume? That evening she bought three more like atomizers at the worker-owned-and-operated hippie perfumery downtown.

About two weeks later – two weeks, two classes, that first hungry look now followed by another, less pleading, more insistent, thus somehow sexier stare – Louise had gathered the courage to approach him after class. She'd waited patiently behind the usual gaggle of long-haired brainy beauties who fluttered around his lectern, rubbing one bare foot with the other far below her vintage miniskirt – it was spring, Louise hated shoes, she padded around campus soles to grass and mud as often as she could. Finally the crowds thinned and she stepped up to him. 'Professor Harrington,' she'd said, 'I'm a little bit confused . . .' 'Maybe there's something we can do about that, Louise,' said Peter. 'Perhaps we can have a cup of coffee and discuss your confusion for a while,' and her stomach had dropped, and her knees had knocked together. A professor was coming on to her. Was this kind of behavior allowed? She loved how naughty it felt. Two cups of coffee later, plus a happy hour in Collegetown, and Louise had somehow found herself curled like spoons with Peter, back in the single bed of her single dorm room. After, she'd dared to ask what had provoked the high-beam action in class – was it the perfume, the way the light from the window graced her auburn head, could he sense somehow that as girls go, now, with Scott Feinstadt gone she was one of the saddest? – for up until this encounter, at college Louise had felt vaporous and invisible, as if even her physical movement through space caused no disturbance of the surrounding molecules, as if in terms of both form and content she were incapable of stirring the air. It was a feeling somewhat akin to the feeling she experienced almost two decades later, that very morning, for example, when she'd walked by all those carefree students and made her way to the admissions department and her office, unseen by any of them.

But back then, her invisibility was happily cured. She and Peter had done nothing if not stir up the stagnant air in her little dorm room, for the young Peter was a determined lover, a determinedly sensitive lover – he'd read books! – and she was in the mood to be flattered a little; she was in the mood to be loved by her professor. How smart he was then to accommodate her, for that very night, scrunched together under her single feather-weight comforter, a box of graham crackers open and crumbly between them, when gently pressed, Peter confessed to having noticed her right along. Louise couldn't believe her luck.

'The fawn.' That's what Peter confided to Louise he had taken to calling her – daring the cookie crumbs, pulling her moist, soft skin a little closer, burying his words like a string of prayers into the back of her white neck. For months he'd called her that, while sitting up late nights with his best friend and housemate, Derrick, two junior professors endlessly debating the ethics of fucking a student. After one such scotch-soaked night with Derrick – the fawn! the fawn! – Derrick retired (gratefully) to the safety of the computer lab, leaving Peter alone and staring for hours at the endless Ithaca rain falling romantically outside their steamed-up windows, while he built up his resolve. And then it occurred to him, he'd always gone after what he'd wanted before: No guts, no glory!, said Peter, now recounting his change of heart, in her bed, into the curve of her neck, the moisture of his breath leaving behind a delicate necklace of tiny beads as if his lips were pressed up against a piece of glass; somehow he managed to sound sincere. So in class that day he'd taken the plunge, looked up, looked straight into her eyes, Louise's eyes, one of maybe sixty pairs of eyes in the lecture hall, and said his line. 'The calcium in your bones comes from the remnants of dead stars.' The calcium in *her* bones, he'd said it to her, for her; her calcium, her bones, recycled stellar matter, energy neither destroyed nor created, all that grand, poetic, reassuring, Buddhisty, science stuff. For the first time in far too long she'd felt, well, connected somehow, important, a piece of the grand complex concert of the universe, part of life. And so, like many legendary coeds before her, Louise passed the course with flying colors and married the instructor. She was young and nebulous and eager for guidance. He was interesting, accomplished, kind to her. For a while this was enough for both of them.

So there were a whole array of college boys Louise had never really had a chance to sample, boys like the boys who at the moment were cavorting happily outside her office window, boys without cars, boys who served buttered noodles at dinner parties, boys who never seemed to have toilet paper in their bathrooms. Back then, Peter and his roommate, they had kept a box of Tampax under their bathroom sink. That's how evolved they were. Her ex-husband, Peter, gentle, smart, authoritative, wise; this was where she had gone wrong. She'd married a 'catch'. *You should have married a loser?* Her mother quipped inside her head. Maybe, maybe a loser would have allowed Louise herself to shine.

Enough avoidance. Louise looked down at Scott Feinstadt's folder. Who was this mystery MFA applicant with her old boyfriend's moniker? Dare she peek inside?

It had become hot in her office, now, with the windows closed and the sun streaming in. Louise began to sweat. She felt damp beneath her armpits. She reached across her desk for a Kleenex, then held each arm up briefly as she blotted herself dry. The smooth cool pale-vanilla folder slid around her lap like a tiny skiff on a yellow linen sea, but she was able to balance it on her knees enough to keep it from falling over. She tossed the Kleenex into the little olive green wicker trash basket where it blossomed like a white rose. She inhaled deeply and took the plunge.

Feinstadt. F. Scott.

F. Scott? The name was written in at the top of the application in a tight and even hand. Not-typed, of course, but in a rich black ink, perhaps a fountain pen – which her Scott Feinstadt had favored, the wealth and elegance, the dignity of oily ink – the letters had nice full curves to them before they feathered away into nothing. She glanced further down the paragraph. His address was left blank. A post office box. A post office box in Mamaroneck. Mamaroneck, the sister city to her native Larchmont. She read on.

Date of Birth. August 28, 1976.

Her Scott Feinstadt (not an F. Scott Feinstadt) had been born August 28, 1960. She remembered this because he had also died on August 28th – August 28, 1980 – a fact that a lot of people in her town had valued as having some mystical if useless significance, but that she had only found creepy and fitting and somehow round – a kid dying the moment he turned twenty, just as he became a man.

More, there was more. This Scott Feinstadt, *F.* Scott Feinstadt, was just about to graduate from the Rhode Island School of Design. He was a painter and a printmaker. He favored large, oblong canvases, like her Scott Feinstadt had, and he only painted in oils, too, although unlike her guy, he liked to layer the paint with linseed oil until the colors melted slightly under its weight, 'like brown sugar burning', said his essay. He liked to 'caramelize the hues'. F. Scott Feinstadt had also spent a year in Italy, where he had exhausted most of his time 'eating gelati, drinking wine and looking at art, sitting in churches, spending my Bar Mitzvah money'. There was an ironic edge to his essay; it was gently self-mocking but full of self-love as well. 'I believe in myself. I guess you could say I believe in

myself totally. There's *a ton* I need to learn, but I believe that
I have the ability to apprentice myself, to grow by leaps and
bounds. I want to live wildly and adventurously, which might
be interpreted as hubris, but is honestly the way I feel about
myself.'

F. Scott Feinstadt had three recommendation letters, two
from the high priest and priestess of RISD, and one from
Louise's very own tenth grade art teacher. Ms Cipriani. 'In my
thirty years of teaching, Scott is one of the top five most gifted
young artists I have ever seen ... blah blah ... and while
I don't normally approve of high school students painting
nudes from live models, Scott's portrait of a girlfriend is
reminiscent of one of Matisse's cruder odalisques.'

Louise was reeling. Berta, Trisha, Theresa Longo, all of
his exes, captured in full flower, their finest hour, at the
art show of the senior class. It was a town scandal, Rabbi
and Mrs Feinstadt loyally at their son's side holding their
heads high, the girls aflutter, instant celebrities. Her Scott
Feinstadt had never immortalized her own naked, nubile
image – he'd promised, but had never gotten around to it.
He'd rather (his words) make love to her than reduce her to
a work of art.

'I give him my highest and heartiest recommendation,'
wrote Ms Cipriani.

And, who could believe it, Ms Cipriani, a product of the
'60s – Louise remembered her long sheet of brown hair,
prematurely rusting gray – still signed off her letters with
'in harmony and peace'. Was she out of her mind?

Was Louise?

Louise picked up her phone to call Peter. She still reached

for him when she needed to reach for somebody. Lately it had occurred to her that their divorce had been as gentle and somnambulant as their marriage – they were both kind, decent people, and so they had moved apart kindly and decently and stayed friends with one another and therefore neither had progressed much, which, it also occurred to her, might be part of why she was now so lonely. Still, Louise dialed his extension: three sixes – as if he were more dangerous than he was – and then the more indicting zero.

'Physics,' this year's probably pretty, very young, work-study student answered the phone, and, a beat later, as if the connection were hiccupping its way overseas, her own ex picked up, 'Professor Peter Harrington', his voice steady and full of authority.

Louise was unable to speak. Instead, she gasped, a little liquidy gasp as if she were gulping air down fast, to keep from crying.

'Mrs Harrington?' said the work-study girl. 'Is that you again?'

'That's all right, Farrah,' said Peter, and Louise heard Farrah hang up the line.

Farrah. Clearly, this child of God was older than Louise had assumed, probably a grad student, one who had been out in the world a bit, for obviously she had been conceived during the heyday of the TV show *Charlie's Angels*. When they'd first started out, Peter's rosters had had a smattering of Samanthas and Tabithas. Her last batch of grad school applications were crammed full of Alexises and Crystals, more illegitimate offspring of Aaron Spelling. Was a generation of Toris lurking around the corner?

'Lou,' said Peter, 'are you all right?'

Louise nodded. She nodded across the line. She nodded that she was fine, when she was not fine, even though she was going out of her mind.

'Are we still on for dinner?'

Of course, thought Louise. It was a Thursday. Thursdays at her place. If she was too tired to cook – and wasn't she always too tired to cook these days? – she would hunt through the take-out menus, pick up the phone and dial. Peter loved food, and Louise saw it as her duty to keep him satisfied: crystal shrimp dumplings cabbed directly to her apartment from Shun Lee West for an extra twenty dollars; the best uni and tomiko rolls to be found on the Upper West Side; a real Mission-style burrito. Whatever ethnicity would tease his palate, Louise herself would order 'the' salad: Chinese chicken, or seaweed, or avocado and shrimp in a tortilla shell. That was Thursdays. Monday nights, they ate at Peter's. He'd take the subway down to Balducci's for anchovies and capers packed in salt. He'd swing past the Union Square farmer's market and handpick the heirloom tomatoes and edamame and mizuna. Olives and cheese came from Murray's Cheese Shop. The olive oil itself he ordered over the Internet. Bread from the Sullivan Street Bakery. The shopping alone took hours. Then there was the wine, letting it breathe, reading the cork. They almost never sat down to eat until ten o'clock. Each meal he set out to top his last venture. He pored through cookbooks, *Gourmet, Saveur, Food & Wine.* Everything was such a production. Last time it was chicken breaded with panko – Japanese breadcrumbs. Japanese breadcrumbs? Did they even have bread in Japan? Louise, of course, tried to avoid loading up on carbs when she could. Monday nights, she hated him.

'Yes,' said Louise. 'We're on.'

'Good,' said Peter. 'We'll talk about "it" later.' That was Peter, he knew there was an it, and he was confident that this it, like all the other its in her life, could wait. He was confident that nothing new would ever happen to her.

Louise hung up the phone.

She picked it up again. She needed to call someone, but who? She was bursting. Her mother? No way. Mom had barely tolerated the original Scott Feinstadt. *A pretty boy good-for-nothing.* What would she make of the second? Missy. She could call Missy, her old high school friend, the one who had stolen Scott Feinstadt right out from under her.

It had taken them a while to reconcile, Louise and Missy, former best pals for life, blood sisters even, from their days of pajama parties and all-girl make-outs. There were six of them back then, Louise and Missy, Mindy and Lori, Rachel and Sabelle, and one ring leader, Anna, who would pair her pupils off, sit the girls cross-legged in a semicircle and instruct them in the art of kissing. All Louise could bear to remember now were her lips on Missy's cloud of black hair, her entire sensory being awash in an overpowering, slippery haze of Herbal Essence, searching furtively for Missy's neck. Later, in their teen years, childhood sexual play magically forgotten, they were confidantes and late-night callers, Cheese Bazaar regulars and Loehmann's shoppers. Nothing had hurt Louise more, maybe not even Scott's death (for hadn't he just a little bit gotten what he'd deserved?), than the sight of Scott and Missy climbing out of his truck and walking arm and arm down White Plains Road, each with one hand buried in the butt pocket of the other's blue jeans, while she, Louise, totally alone (and – sigh – waiting at the bus stop) still loved him.

She had felt a similar feeling, of loss coupled with the shock of emotional continuation, when at twenty-four, newly married and amorous, she'd found herself pregnant, and then almost immediately, not. Louise hadn't had much time to think a lot about said baby, or what it possibly could have meant to her, or even if she wanted one, except simply to realize when she'd lost it that she loved it. She was so young then, everybody said; everybody said there would be more babies, and she'd believed them, for wasn't she just a tiny little baby then herself? And so it had surprised Louise in the coming weeks to find that she still charted the pregnancy in her head, and on the day of her baby's projected birth she was somehow surprised, again, to find herself still childless. It surprised her still, childlessness did. The persistence of it. That this particular baby had turned out to have been her only chance.

Louise had continued to love Scott Feinstadt in the same futile but enduring way she had continued to love her baby, even though there was no baby, even though Scott Feinstadt had stopped loving her, even though that bitch Missy had won out. The day of his funeral – *What a scene!* – Mom had accompanied her out of both maternal instinct and, Louise suspected, mordant curiosity. Missy sat in the front pew on the right side of Rabbi and Mrs Feinstadt, while Scott's sisters, Stacey and Annie, held them up from the left, a set of curly-haired girlish bookends. From time to time Missy had turned her tear-stained face around to survey the crowd, and,

Louise was sure, to gloat. It had taken two years, nine months and thirty-five days after that (that being her first night with Peter) for Louise to forgive Missy enough to return her calls. They had been on the phone off and on ever since.

Now Missy was living in L.A. A retired development person (a 'D-Girl'), she was married to a sexy Bolivian writer/director and with the help of in-vitro fertilization she had given birth to twins: Owen and Olivia. She'd traded in her Jil Sander suits for Earl jeans, her breakfasts at Hugo's for mothers' groups. She'd grown her curly black hair long again, and it was more tangly now than when they were kids. How odd that after such a glamorous twenties, and this was true of so many people that Louise knew, in her late thirties, Missy returned to the sartorial choices of her teens, while Louise, despite some chiding from her ex-husband, continued to blow whatever pittance she earned on anything that might make her look like she was invited to great parties. As Louise saw it, faithfully following the current season was a clear sign of who – in these first shocking years of being not-young – was feeling desperate, and who was not. I.e., Louise had spent the last few weeks of winter all in red, the new black. She was spending these first few weeks of spring in yellow and Indian pink, the new whites. She'd exercised her body until even those little spare chins under her arms, her arm flaps!, now were as hard as rock. Missy, on the other hand, had spent their previous two phone calls extolling the virtues of Dr Blue Jeans, a man who could take even her most tattered but beloved pair of dungarees from high school (when Missy was still on the zaftig side) and restore them into something gentle and wearable. Poochy Missy, with the help of Dr Blue Jeans, slipping back into her low-waisted old boot-legged Levi's, proudly displaying the status symbol of the moment, the soft, lightly fluted belly of someone who'd borne children. It was hard not to be envious.

'Miss,' Louise said. 'It's me.'

'I hate him. I hate him. I hate him.'

The 'him' of course was Marcos, Missy's husband. She either loved him or hated him, depending on the timing of Louise's call.

'What did he do now?' asked Louise, although who cared? Who in the world cared what Marcos did, besides ICM and CAA and the AAMPS?

American Academy of Motion Picture Sciences.

Sciences?

Who cared, except for a small, elite cadre of reporters at *People* magazine?

'He's at The Ivy, right? With Jay and Marc and a bunch of his producers. And something pisses him off, the old blah blah blah, you know what I'm saying?'

Well, yes, thought Louise. I do know. I guess that's why we're still girlfriends.

'Long story short, Zorro throws the script in Jay's face.'

'God,' said Louise. 'Isn't Jay the one who bailed him out of jail?'

'Yes, only you're not supposed to know that, the jail part, right, you don't know the jail part right, Louise? No one's supposed to know – the tabloids would have a field day. Oh God, don't make me regret now that I told you.'

'Told me what?' said Louise, like a true friend, while picking at a tiny stand of hair on her leg that the waxing stylist must have missed. Anything to have another human's hands touch her. Salt rubs. Seaweed wraps. French manicures with tips.

'I love you,' breathed Missy, breathlessly. 'I love you more than him.' Wasn't that the sad truth about girlfriends, that you loved one another more than you ever did any of your men? But still you'd drop her on a dime for him?

'Oh, Marcos isn't so bad,' said Louise. 'He's just got a temper.'

'Of course he has a temper,' said Missy. 'He's Bolivian. He's supposed to have a temper. I married him for his temper. They love him for his temper. Lunch wouldn't be worth the check if he didn't at least throw a script at them.'

She paused.

'Maybe he should have thrown a chair.'

'I don't get it,' said Louise, shifting forward in her seat. 'I thought you were mad . . . I thought he was rude . . .'

'He came home without the cheesecake,' said Missy. 'I never get to go anywhere. I'm a hausfrau. I'm worse off than my mother was. I live for his doggie bags.'

Was it true? Was Missy worse off than her mother? Mrs Goldberg had spent the bulk of their teen years trying desperately to 'reestablish herself' after marriage, children and divorce all conspired to knock her legs out from under her – she'd entertained everything from EST to disco hopping to colonics. She'd been newly enrolled in social work school the year she died, Roller blading hand in hand with her twenty-five-year-old boyfriend straight into a Pepperidge Farm truck on the Boston Post Road. Was this the price of illicit, incipient happiness? Louise had met the guy only once, at the reception at Missy's wedding. He'd been a cheerful boy in a rent-a-tux chugging back a beer. After the introductions – 'Meet Chuck, Mom's boy-toy', and some minor awkward pleasantries – 'So you're the best friend . . . cool . . . very cool . . .' – that kind of stuff – he'd winked conspiratorially at Louise and said: 'I know none of you can understand what Mrs Goldberg sees in me . . .' – did he really say 'Mrs Goldberg', Louise wondered now, interrupting her own recollections, or was it just the child in her still dictating all her memories? – 'but she's been around the block enough by now to know that us guys don't get any more mature, she might as well have us while our bodies are still good.' At the time, Louise had found the line funny but sad. Now she couldn't quite fathom what had been so sad about it. They'd had about four blissful months, Mrs Goldberg and her Chuck, which seemed pretty good, in retrospect. At least, Missy said, they went out on a high. And so, to the chagrin of the boy's parents, but as an example of what was right with her, Missy had managed to bury them side by side.

'Anyways,' Missy was whispering now. 'I wrote Roger a letter.'

'Who?' said Louise.

'Roger, my old boyfriend from college.'

'The financial analyst?'

'Exactly. He must have made scads of money by now, he's got five kids, all girls, and he's living in Greenwich.'

'How do you know all this?' asked Louise.

'I had Marcos look up his website. So I wrote him this real cute, chatty, informal note, saying I'd just gotten some stupid alumni something or other, and well, you know, I thought of him.' Missy sighed. 'He can take it from there, don't you think?'

Always the bold one.

'Did you mail it?'

'Marcos mailed it for me.'

'Marcos mailed it?'

'After I read it to him.'

'You read it to him?'

'Yeah, and you know what he said?'

'Noooo . . .'

'He said: "I healous o dis guy . . ."'

Why did Missy always sound like Lucy doing Ricky when she was doing Marcos?

'So, it worked,' Louise interrupted, growing increasingly impatient.

'No, I never got to finish the rest of the sentence, you keep interrupting me.'

'I'm sorry,' said Louise, sounding injured.

'Don't sound injured, Louise,' said Missy. 'Marcos said, "I healous o dis guy cause he got out when the getting was goot."'

Both women stopped to contemplate the sentence.

'I hate him,' said Missy.

'I'm at work, Miss,' said Louise.

'You are? God, how was I to know? You didn't even reverse the charges.'

'I'll talk to you later.'

Click.

Louise hung up, a bit dizzy and feeling lost. For a minute she didn't know what day it was, or why she'd dialed Missy in the first place. Missy could do that for her. Disorient her. Which was why Louise loved her.

Louise looked down at her desk. She knocked on it. It was solid. It definitely was her new desk, her inherited mess, officially her office. Right in the middle of it all was F. Scott Feinstadt's application, exactly where she'd left it. F. Scott Feinstadt, his essay and his stats. And two phone numbers: area code 401 until the end of this week and then 516. No guts, no glory, right, Pete? Right? Without hesitating, Louise picked up the receiver and dialed. The phone rang one time, two times, three; exhausted, she almost rested the receiver in its cradle. But she persisted, she hung in there. Four rings, five rings, six. On the seventh, someone picked up.

'Hey,' said a mysterious young man.

'Hey yourself,' said Louise.

Why on earth did she say that?

'Baby,' he said.

'This is Louise Harrington,' Louise said. 'From Columbia University, School of the Arts, admissions.'

'So you're not my baby,' the young man laughed.

No. Apparently not.

'Is this F. Scott Feinstadt?' she asked, all business.

'Yeah,' he said. 'Sure.'

There was silence on the line. Was that really Scott Feinstadt's voice? It sounded vaguely familiar. But after seventeen years, anyone's memory could play tricks – especially after one reached thirty, when, if one were female, which Louise was, definitely female, one could suffer a significant decline in estrogen. Louise's mother, a devoted reader of both *The New England Journal of Medicine* and the supermarket variety of women's magazines, had sent Louise a sheaf of clippings. *Tick, Tick, Tick,* scrawled Mom's note. Helpfully.

'Louise,' said F. Scott Feinstadt. 'Are you still there?'

You better believe it, asshole, Louise thought. I'm right where you left me.

'Yes,' said Louise.

'That's good to know,' said F. Scott.

Was he being kind? Or was he just another jerk?

Funny how, even to this day, she was still not sure in which direction her Scott Feinstadt had swung his pendulum.

'I'm calling to schedule your admissions interview,' Louise said, making the interview up on the spot.

'I didn't know one was required,' said F. Scott.

One wasn't. No one had ever been interviewed during the entire history of the School of the Arts. It would take too much time.

Still.

'It isn't, but if you want your candidacy to be taken seriously, you should have one.' Who was this office Nazi talking on her phone?

'How about next Wednesday, five o'clock?' said F. Scott. 'I'm all wrapped up in my work until then.' A pause. 'And then there's tennis. Okay.'

'Okay,' said Louise. She did not know what else to say. She hung in there on the line anyway. Not quite yet ready to let go of him.

An awkward silence ensued. A very awkward silence.

'I can still hear you breathing,' said F. Scott Feinstadt. 'So if I still have your undivided attention, I've got a confession to make.'

Thunk-thump. A flutter, then the familiar, but always startling, racing of her heart. What was he going to confess? That he was really forty years old? That he worked for the CIA? That this was all an elaborate hoax, the accident, the funeral, her marriage, her life? The topsy-turvy trick of his application? Were they on *Candid Camera? The Truman Show?* Had he read in their high school alumni news that she was now divorced and not getting any, and therefore somehow ripe? For forgiveness? For him? And now, finally, after all these years, twenty, twenty fucking big ones, would he now say, as she imagined he could, in her own private Idaho, in the soft, tender white tissue, the vulnerable little clam belly of her soul: 'It was all a hideous mistake, babe. Dumping you. Playing dead. The truth is, you're the only one I ever loved.'

Could dreams, indeed, come true?

She'd have to ask Peter. He was the scientist. Therefore, he had always been the partner with faith in magic.

'You're not going to believe this, but I was just about to pick up the phone and call,' said F. Scott. 'I forgot to send in my slides. This must be some weird psychic phenomenon, you know?'

'You're telling me,' Louise said.

———◆———

That night, Peter and Louise sat cross-legged in Louise's living room, on the floor, eating their dinner Japanese-style off of her coffee table. They did this basically because Louise had no dining room – just a living room box, and a bedroom box, that fed off of a kitchen and bathroom box, respectively. No hallways, no moldings, no foyers, no flow. *A palace.* Still, Louise was lucky to have it, this apartment – at more than half her monthly salary – now that she was no longer a bona fide University spouse. She had no status left. And no table or chairs. All her earnings were going toward her wardrobe. Haircuts. Highlighting. The visual upkeep of her self and spirit, what she wore to face the outside world. Since she was the one to actually move out – Peter packing all her art in bubble wrap, her books and dishes for her, practically sweeping her along with her dust right out the door – and the dining room set had come origi-nally from his mother's basement, they'd both deemed it only fair that he keep the faux Chippendale, a piece she'd always hated. Now, four years after moving out on her own, Louise and her one guest (Peter) were still eating on the floor.

He was telling her about his day. How he'd proceeded through his tasks – a lecture, a department head meeting, a faculty lunch, which proved to be inedible, mayonnaisey – at such and such a velocity. How a drop in his blood sugar had forced him at 2 PM into an abrupt stop. The force of which knocked him back in time. For a moment, said Peter, rather cockily, he'd felt young. For a moment, crossing the quad, on the way back to his building, his pressure dropping, feeling light, he thought he was 'one of the them.' He imagined himself in cutoff jeans. Astronomy was his first love again.

The earth smelled clean and green. And all the girls looked pretty. His head was full of stars.

Peter looked down at Louise's mock Oriental as he spoke. His voice had been full of the ironic edge he had picked up over the years – when had Peter become ironic? – but now from the angle of his bent head she could tell that he was in fact being genuine. And he did seem younger now, somehow, to Louise, younger and more vulnerable than usual, a little bit less than fully in control – which was so odd and un-Peter-like that she had to look away. He reminded her of himself when she'd first met him, when he'd teetered on the cusp of man and kid.

'I guess it must have been spring fever,' said Peter, referring to his earlier youth-jolt. 'That's what Farrah thought.'

Farrah? The work-study student? Farrah 'thought'?

Spring fever. Maybe. Maybe pollen had gotten the best of her. Maybe Scott Feinstadt and F. Scott Feinstadt were mere figments of her imagination. Maybe as chimeras go, they were a pair of Irish twins. Louise had been looking for a way to broach the F. Scott Feinstadt business with Peter all evening. But for the life of her she couldn't find the best approach. What was she supposed to say, 'The boy I loved before you, that young, handsome, talented, exciting wild child, has finally come back to claim me?' Or: 'Honey, I believe that I am insane and you should probably have me put on lithium?' And let's face it, Peter's own little nostalgic reverie had struck her as so sadly 'middle-aged' . . . is that how Peter would see her, now, if she bothered to confess? Louise couldn't bear it if he did.

Oh, they had a long history together, Louise and Peter, but

whoever thought they would end up where they both were now? After Cornell, there had been a visiting professorship at Berkeley and from there Peter had found himself soundly placed in the academic firmament; over the years his talents had taken them all over the world, which Louise had initially loved, but grown to despise, why? Why? Why, when in so many, many ways, theirs was the life she had aspired to? The academic rigor, the rootlessness of travel, Peter always smart, always kind. The doors he opened for her; the exotic worlds she entered. Why, her inaugural trip to Europe had been when Peter had squirreled her away with him that very first semester to a talk he was giving in Paris. It had all felt so grown-up. So sophisticated, even elegant. When had it become so empty? When had the red neon sign begun to blink, was it in one of their various faculty apartments when on their third anniversary Peter had traveled alone to a speaking engagement and Louise hadn't at all minded? The conferences had multiplied, and more and more Peter was booking a series of solo flights. But in the beginning he'd lead the way, she'd pack the bags, his tweedy professor clothes, his running shorts, several packages of condoms, her Ann Taylor office garb for the various administrative office jobs some dean would dream up for her at whatever university where Peter was holding court; she'd fold her little black cocktail dresses and tuck away her good string of pearls for the conferences and award dinners and presentations, for the trips to Washington D.C., the stints at NASA, for whatever college had wooed him away that particular semester, wearing them to the art openings and fundraisers she'd make it her business to curate as she followed him from one academic constellation to another, when the intellectual stimulation still carried her along, even after she stopped her Trojan-buying trips to the drugstore. She'd been a good wife; curious, supportive, intelligent. Peter had been a good husband. And still, with all their good intentions and fine ingredients, the romance in their marriage had slowly and mysteriously leaked out, replaced by some heavy, invisible, colorless, tasteless cosmic gas.

On their eighth anniversary, her girlfriend Missy had sent them a card from her hacienda in the Hollywood Hills: Here's to four good years.

It was a joke, of course, and not a particularly generous one, but that card led Louise to thinking that day about why, after brushing her teeth and having her orange juice in the morning, (a) she had a dreadful taste in her mouth and (b) all she ever wanted to do was crawl back into bed again.

It took two more years to get out of it. That was four years ago, two years since Missy had started fixing her up with guys who conveniently lived on another coast, guys who would call her for drinks when they came in to town 'to get a culture fix' and then never call again, ten years since Peter and Louise had first been married. What had happened to the bright, young, happy couple they once were?

She looked up at a painting, framed and hanging over her nonworking fireplace. Throughout her apartment, the rest of her precious art collection – the smattering of prints, etchings, woodcuts, that she'd picked up on their travels or for a pittance from various students at various colleges – hung on her walls. Wandering Jews trailed from a series of terra-cotta pots sitting precariously atop the sills, Bonsais had been trained on the shelving in the kitchen, and in the bathroom, on the narrow enamel ledge that framed the chest-high tiled section of her walls, squatted half a dozen half-burnt votives in Moroccan lanterns she'd bartered for herself in a market in Marrakech. Instead of curtains, shimmery, pale, purple Indian saris that they'd collected during a sabbatical to Calcutta were draped artfully across her bedroom window, and her stereo and a smattering of Peter's opera CDs cluttered up the only bit of native charm in the whole place, that same plaster mantle encrusted in pink paint, like layer upon layer of calamine lotion – she'd spent an entire weekend trying to strip it down when she'd first moved in. The university life: Louise still lived like a professor's wife. But this painting, her prize possession, her 'poem without words', this one was special to her, an oil. It had been made expressly for her by Scott Feinstadt – actually, it had been ferreted out of the detritus that marred his 'studio' in the synagogue basement when he was packing up for school – and given to her as a parting gesture, after the breakup, after Missy, before his lionization, when Scott Feinstadt was still alive and kicking and terribly guilt-ridden (she was a crier then, Louise, constantly welling up and tearing over in his presence), when Scott Feinstadt was still capable of proving what a mensch he was.

It wasn't half bad, Scott's painting; it was almost kind of great even, for a kid, for a kid without a lot of technique or life experience, for a kid who'd spent not quite a year in Italy, in Europe. She knew this, for isn't that how she passed her days at Columbia, evaluating youthful potential, searching for that certain *je ne sais quoi*, that extra special spark? The image was, he said, 'an abstract mother and child'. Not bad at all. It wasn't truly terrible or anything, that is for someone who didn't really know from churches, from icons, not bad for a nice Jewish boy from Larchmont, a rabbi's son, who'd spent his last nine months staring at paintings of the Baby Jesus and His Mother. It was even kind of beautiful, Louise thought now, looking at the painting for the zillionth time, the darkness of it, the heaviness of the oils deepening the greens, blacks and blues. You could feel the maternal love blossoming forth, surrounding Him, like an aching, tender bruise.

What it showed was promise.

'What are you looking at, Lou?' asked Peter.

'Scott Feinstadt's painting,' said Louise.

'The best thing about our divorce,' Peter said. 'That you got custody. I always hated it.' He rolled his eyes at her when he said it. The best thing. Was he as lonely now as she was?

'Sammy called today.'

Sammy, Louise's younger brother.

'Another business proposition, although this one sounds like a good investment. I was thinking, if we pooled together a little of our money . . .'

What money? thought Louise. She'd just spent sixty dollars on eye cream.

'What money?' said Louise. 'I don't have any money. And should we really put any nonexistent money in a Sammy scheme?'

'I've been putting a little extra away for you,' said Peter. His gaze was sure and steady. 'Ever since my pay raise.'

There was silence.

'You've got to be kidding,' said Louise. 'What are you, my fucking father?'

Peter's eyes narrowed. 'Clearly, not, Louise.'

'Then why did you put money away for me?'

'I put money away for you because you neglect to do it for yourself,' said Peter.

'How can you be so patronizing?' said Louise.

'I prefer the term "pragmatic",' said Peter.

For a moment Louise just sat and stewed.

'Look, Lou, it's stupid to turn down a good opportunity out of stubborness and pride.

'Stubborness? Pride?'

'Sammy's idea, it's intriguing as ideas go . . . I'll know more later in the week. He and I are having lunch.'

Louise was afraid that she might scream. He was putting money away for her like she was an incompetent. And Sammy? The nerve of him. Trying to fleece her ex? The horror of it all must have shown on her face, right then, because Peter quickly tried to steer away the conversation.

'Let it go for now, Lou.'

'Let it go?'

'Yes,' said Peter, definitively. Authoritatively. 'I don't want to fight with you.'

'What if I want to fight?' said Louise.

'It takes two,' said Peter, softly.

That was the trouble, it did take two, to fight, sure, it took two for so many things they were no longer any good at.

'So, ah, what was bothering you earlier today?' Peter asked, deflecting, sure, but with more than a crumb of authentic curiosity. That was the trouble with Peter, with hating him, or at least disengaging from him. In his own way, he was honestly concerned. The good news was that he would be incapable of doing anything about whatever troubled her.

'Oh, you know,' said Louise, giving in.

But he didn't. Who could?

'It was Missy. And her marriage. She's purposefully trying to stir the pot.'

Peter glazed over. Other people's problems were not his forte. He liked something he could fix. An overdrawn checking account, a car engine, physics theorems, planning his ex-wife's life for her – *Do you think he's trying to absolve himself of guilt? What guilt, Mom?* What in the world did Peter Harrington have to feel guilty about? Besides making Louise feel like an idiot?

Peter nodded, made a couple of cracks at Missy's expense for Louise's sake, but basically, thankfully, he tuned out. It was this ability to be both physically present and emotionally absent that had kept them together for so long, even after they weren't really together any longer. The lack of challenge had been a godsend.

After about twenty minutes, Louise steered the conversation back to him and the rest of his day.

'So did it last?' Louise asked, meanly. 'Your youthful euphoria?' She was trying to irk him, but she also really did want to know.

'No,' said Peter, cracking a smile. 'As soon as I saw that pile of ungraded undergraduate exams waiting on my desk, I was old again . . .'

Still, a latte from the new coffee cart that had been set up in the lobby of his building (capital improvements! the product of a rising endowment!) along with his requisite five sugars, brought upstairs to him, unrequested and out of simple thoughtfulness by the devoted Farrah *(again, Farrah?)*, had brightened up his day.

'Gotta love that new dean,' said Peter. 'They even stock Krispy Kremes. Farrah brought me a chocolate custard.'

Mmmm.

Louise picked at her soba salad, limp and gray with a smattering of fluorescent green confetti – it was either chopped-up Easter grass or seaweed. Farrah and her Krispy Kremes. In Louise's apartment there were no grams of fat, no fat grams around for miles. She sucked a blade of the green stuff out from between her teeth. *What the hell kind of a name is Farrah, anyway? Dutch? Lebanese?*

Louise was on her own.

For a week, Louise Harrington could neither eat nor sleep. She lost three pounds. She didn't get her work done, but mooned dreamily out her window. She started pulling her shoulder-length hair, now artfully highlighted at Bumble & Bumble, back over her forehead and fastening it with a clip, wearing it the way her Scott Feinstadt had always favored, little tendrils of curls wisping around her forehead. Finally, on a Tuesday evening, after work, she broke down and took the train from Grand Central station up to Larchmont and her mother's house, with the intention of going through her old boxes. It had been a long day at the office, a long day of looking out the window, of wild sexual fantasies and wondering if she'd lost her mind. She had taken two subway lines plus the shuttle to get herself across town. She'd been so late and frazzled that she'd had to sprint – sprint as fast as the clogs she'd unearthed from her closet would let her (they were back in style; the art students at school were now wearing them, as they were wearing the Adidas and skinny striped sweaters and vintage beading of her youth) – rather she'd clattered racketously down the gateway ramp (she'd forgotten how to walk in them, the Manolo Blahniks she'd picked up at a sample sale she could manage, but clogs?) and sunk deep into her musty, torn seat, the scent of sweat and old semen rising up to meet her, just as the train pulled out down the long, dark, rank tunnel. Rats lived in there, she was sure.

Louise shut her eyes. She shut her eyes against the darkness, and then again, after a quick blink, kept them shut against the smoggy, gray light of Harlem and the elevated train line. She kept her eyes shut for the twenty minutes or so it took that silverfish of a train to slide out of the City into air that smelled green when the doors again finally slid open, when the moist, warm, fertile blast of trees and mold and puddles and soil entered the car and she could breathe, when the train came to a stop. It was only when the Metro North had left one world and entered another, when she was safely over the bridge that spanned her two separate universes, when she shed her urban skin for her suburban one, that Louise dared to open her eyes. Houses and trees. Wasn't that why her parents had moved there in the first place? Who was she to question a wisdom such as theirs? It was another twenty minutes, then, to her birthplace, to Larchmont.

—◆—

Mom was waiting behind the front door, nose pressed up against the screen. A little silver-bobbed spitfire, much tinier and more solid than Louise – 'a live wire in a pantsuit', that's how Scott Feinstadt had described her, although now of course she didn't wear pantsuits, she wore bad DKNY from the sales racks at Loehmann's, all the off colors, orange and puce and chartreuse, she wore Liz Sport, and Ellen Tracy, and a little of her spark had leaked out in the last seventeen years, not a lot, but enough, just a little. Louise had noticed. Now, at this exact moment, Mom wore Mom jeans, so she looked less like a live wire, and more like a stubby little supermarket candle, the color on the label termed 'denim', her silver head a small, sleek wick. She must have been back early from the VA hospital, Louise thought, with time enough to change out of her workaday outfit and get ready for a *rare* visit from her daughter. Who needs to visit, countered Louise, you're always nattering, nattering, nattering, in my head? Even with Louise at the controls, Mom couldn't shut up.

—◆—

Ellie Silverstein was a discharge planner. She spent her days finding home health care workers and specials on colostomy bags for her HMO-dependent, too-soon-to-be-sent-home patients – most of whom were elderly. Like her girl Louise, Mom had planned her own career around her now ex-husband's job. He was a doctor, Louise's dad. Retired and living down in Florida, where he appeared remotely happy – 'remote' being the key word – with his second wife, a surgical nurse, *every cliché in the book, of course, your father never had an original bone in his body* (original 'bone', thought Louise, original 'bone'?) and his wife's two juvenile delinquent children. Louise flew down to see them all every spring break of her adult life, often finding herself on the same cheapie flight as a smattering of her work-study students. Once Peter came along too, even after the divorce, for a little r & r, a freebie vacation, to burn his scalp, he said, and toast his nose, eat some good Miami deli – basically to keep her company. Louise hated to admit it, but when Peter first offered to accompany her she'd allowed herself to get just a little bit excited. Whenever Louise felt especially lonely, she used to fantasize about their hooking up again; it made sense sometimes, in the dark at night, when she was alone, aging away in her apartment, allergic to sleep, since they'd never seemed to have properly unhooked anyway, since Peter was still so smart and so handsome, since he seemed so permanently attached to her, but this trip had proved to be a defining moment. There was the awkward convenience of twin beds in her parents' guest room when they retired that first evening; and when Peter had emerged from the bathroom he'd been dressed in . . . pajamas. It was hard to imagine a moment in her life when she'd felt worse. After that, she made all her trips home on her own.

Now, there was Mom Silverstein, standing anxiously at the door, waiting for her, with fear in her heart; *I hope you wore your seatbelt — remember Princess Di?* But when the taxi stopped, Mom let the screen door slam and moved along back inside. Probably to put up the coffee, probably to feign some mild form of normal indifference in an effort to present herself to the world (Louise and the taxi driver — Mom's world) as a regular mother. Louise paid, and climbed up the slate step walk that circled around back to the kitchen door. Sammy had laid it when, in the midst of taking a year off from college, he had found himself suddenly bereft of funds. The stone fireplace in the living room, the 'new' (seventeen years new) railing on the staircase, the slightly tilted wooden deck out back, were all remnants of this penurious period. Their mother thought it best to pay him for work done around the house, rather than send him out hunting, *hopelessly, recklessly, placing himself in danger,* for a real job — he'd been threatening to go to Alaska and work on a fishing boat. This *craziness* cemented his workfare status. Louise thought it another ploy on both their parts, mother and son, to keep him at home, to infantilize him. And to some degree it had worked — Sammy kept coming back like a homing pigeon. Now newly divorced himself, thirty-three years old and recently returned from rehab, Sammy was in Westchester again. In a huge house in Scarsdale, all by himself, his only furniture a black leather couch, a foosball table and a huge wide-screen TV. Daily, the financial genius, that idiot savant, Sammy, took the same commuter rail Louise had just disembarked from into the City. He was starting a new job. A new life. An old buddy from B-school had wangled Sammy a job as a financial analyst at Goldman Sachs – as long as he kept his mouth shut about the last six months: 'Tell them you were in Tibet, or something,' said the buddy, 'tell them you were fucking finding yourself.' *At least someone around here knows how to make money.* Louise didn't totally like him, Sammy, but she didn't totally dislike him either. The five years between their births had made each of them an only child. What it was was that she didn't exactly, totally trust him. Not since the time when he was in his teens, soon after Scott Feinstadt's death, when she was wiggy around cars anyway and he was still underage, for God's sake, when he'd stolen and wrecked her VW bug. Not since their mother made her instantly forgive him. *He could have broken his neck! Hasn't he suffered enough?* Well, no, thought Louise. Then as well as now, for all his travails, Sammy never seemed to suffer enough.

Peter and Sammy, they'd always managed to get along. Baseball, the stock market, some polite, seductive physics questioning from Sammy that would flatter Peter's narcissism. Boy talk. Louise thought back to Sammy's proposed scheme, whatever it was, and shuddered. Every cell in her body rebelled against it – Peter's behaving more like a guardian for a retarded adult (her!) than even an inordinately friendly ex-husband, Sammy taking Peter for a dupe. She hoped Peter the scientist, not the businessman, wasn't stupid enough to fall for it.

Louise entered through the back door. Decaf coffee was indeed brewing on the shelf. A low-fat coffee ring sat sliced and ready to go in its box. Two mugs: one dented and sporting the logo I Got Smashed in L.A. (a souvenir from Sammy's return-from-rehab party) and one embossed: World's Greatest

Mom, sat side by side on the round kitchen table. It was no big surprise which mug was Louise's mug. She headed straight for the smashed one, and for the little moo-cow creamer, stopping along the way to give her mother's bent head a little kiss. Mom was chopping some onions for supper by the sink. Onions. While she was serving cake. She kept dipping her knife in the running faucet, but still her eyes were full of tears.

'To what do I owe this little visit?' her mother said.

'I don't know, Mom, I guess I just felt like going home.'

'That's why you still have a home to come home to,' said Mom. 'So you can.'

'Where's the kid?' asked Louise. 'Working?'

'Like a dog,' said Mom, and sighed. 'I was so glad that you married an academic. Someone with time for his family. Unlike that goddamn bum.'

Which bum was that, exactly? Louise went quickly down the checklist. Sammy? No. He'd just gone through a *bad spell. Give the poor kid a break.* No bumhood for her Sammy. Louise caught her breath. Her heart was racing. Scott Feinstadt. Or F. Scott Feinstadt. Could it be F. Scott Feinstadt to whom Mom was now referring? Louise felt like her heart and lungs were breaking up into a thousand tiny little puzzle pieces. Her hands began to tremble. She leaned over and pressed them into the worn Formica countertop to steady herself. Was Mom really all-knowing?

It was possible, Louise thought, wasn't it, her head bent forward, on the verge of hyperventilation, that Mom, at this late stage of her life, was in such expert command of her powers, in such top Mom-form that she was capable of just such an early strike, and had already begun her campaign against the newest model of the original bum who had so long ago broken her daughter's heart. Ruined her life really, it seemed to Louise only now in this very second. This horrifying, yet somehow comforting revelation had never occurred to her before – comforting in that now there would be an excuse for how hard and bitter she'd become! there would a reason! – but then again, Scott Feinstadt had never bothered to return from the dead before; truly he had long ago even stopped peopling her dreams.

Or was Mom just being Mom, unforgiving, wrinkling time, still railing on about an affair Louise had had at the tail end of her marriage as if it were yesterday, with a good-for-nothing, getting-older jazz musician, who was always on tour, never around, and still managed to give her the clap?

Nope, none of the above. One look up from the countertop at the all-too-familiar way Mom's eyebrows knit together and it was clear; the bum in question was the bum.

Dad. Well, what did it matter, sighed Louise, palms sweating, breath slowing, heartbeat striving for a normal pace, now that both of them were divorced. What did it matter what kind of hours their respective bums kept? Mom and Louise were both alone now. Period. They were alone, save for what they had with one another.

They were never alone.

'Mom?'

'Hmmm?'

'What ever happened to the Feinstadts?' Louise knew she was tempting fate here, for they rarely discussed the Feinstadts, they had put the whole terrible episode aside, they had gotten on with it, thank God, and now, here Louise was, planting clues, laying bait, potentially whetting Mom's appetite, her nose for trouble – but Louise was desperate. Perhaps F. Scott Feinstadt was Scott Feinstadt's love child, or, more palatably, a distant cousin. If anyone could ferret out the hows and whys, Mom could.

'Well, let's see,' said Mom, not meeting Louise's eyes, purposefully it seemed (Louise knew her), pretending a certain amount of innocent disinterest by concentrating furiously on opening a can of stewed chickpeas, while behind the screen of her silver bangs the wheels in Mom's head began to turn: *Why is she asking about them now?* 'One of the girls married well, some lawyer up in Boston. I think she had a baby. The other didn't. She's a "lesbian".' Mom fairly shouted out the word – she was open-minded. 'I hear she's much more interesting than the lawyer's wife, which just goes to show you, right? She writes books or cooks, or both, I think. I think that Feinstadt girl writes cookbooks. Stacey. Stacey Feinstadt, that's the author. The little one.'

'And Rabbi Feinstadt?'

'They retired to Florida. Not far from your father. Poor Rachel. She never got over her loss. Who could blame her? Still, from the way she carried on about his artistic genius, you would have thought that boy was something special.'

The ire of a spurned girl's mother. It was limitless. Defying death and decades and protocol, common charitable behavior. He'd hurt her Louise, so Mom hated him.

'*Mom,*' said Louise, even after all those years, even now, out of loyalty. Still defending him.

'I suppose it's the worst thing that could happen to a woman,' conceded Mom, meaning Scott, of course. 'The

Feinstadts come back to Larchmont to visit once in a while; they never sold the house – they rent it out to some yuppie couple, with one of those big dogs? I don't get it. If you want a horse, buy a horse. She's always cordial when I see her, Rachel, but she's never regained her bloom. As a young girl, she was lovely.'

Bloom. Is that how Louise would have categorized Scott's mother, as a lovely young girl with a bloom? At the time, back in high school, she'd seen Mrs Feinstadt only as a rival and an impediment. A bright, blue-eyed woman with a wedge haircut, wary of the many girls who entertained her son. A boy's mother. Once, when they were hanging out in the Feinstadt's Florida room, Scott had picked his mother up, thrown her over his shoulder, and deposited her, flirty and laughing and incredibly pleased with herself, on the sofa, right next to Louise. If she'd had a gun, Louise would have shot her. Why couldn't Mrs Feinstadt act her age? Louise had thought back then. Act like a mother, a rabbi's wife, a middle-aged woman. Now, she realized with a start, Louise herself was probably close to the same age at this exact moment that Rachel Feinstadt had been at the time.

All of a sudden, Louise couldn't stand her own skin. She couldn't stand standing in her mother's kitchen. She was thirty-eight years old, pushing forty. What was she doing, still envying Scott Feinstadt's mother? What did Mrs Feinstadt have over her, anyway?

He'd come out of her womb. He'd nestled at her breast. One couldn't break up with one's mother. She should know.

Louise felt a little sick. 'I think I'd like to poke around my old room a bit, before dinner, if there's time?'

'Sure, darling. Poke away. It may be a little dusty in there, though, so open the windows before you breathe. Lucille is getting old.'

Lucille, the cleaning lady. She'd been around longer than Louise had. Why, one of Louise's earliest memories had been watching the Martin Luther King assassination on TV while a sobbing Lucille fluffed pillows in her parents' bedroom.

'Dust paves the way for pneumonia, you know. You can never be too careful.'

Louise exited the kitchen and took the new staircase with the Oriental runner two steps at a time.

———◆———

It was an amazing feeling, entering her childhood room, a scary, exciting, disconcerting sensation, even though the room had been altered over the years and was now a repository for sewing and books and all of Mom's old magazines – the *Ladies Home Journal*s, the *Psychology Today*s, *The Worker, Ms.* magazine. It was, indeed, dusty in the room, so Louise obediently threw open a window before taking her first breath, realizing as she did that now every time she entered a dusty room for the rest of her life she'd think: This paves the way for pneumonia. Everything had changed and still there was a feeling of familiarity; the dotted Swiss curtains, the twin wooden beds, the pale, pale yellow almost-white wallpaper that reminded her so strongly of her childhood. Louise went lightheaded, wavering in the lack of breeze, as

if she might fall to her knees and weep. Instead, she headed
directly for her closet, opened the door, and perused the racks.
Her mother had arranged the various treasures and leftovers
in size order. First things first; Louise pawed through her
most beloved outfits – the burnt-orange velveteen flower-girl
gown she'd worn to her cousin's wedding when she was
six years old. It hung next to the little Swiss mountain girl
dress – complete with dirndl skirt – her parents had brought
home from Europe when she was seven. They were both
packed carefully away in dry-cleaning plastic. Next Louise
met her prepubescent phase head on, the culottes (skorts!)
and balloon pants and pedal pushers, the crocheted matching
vest and mini. (Grandma. Her grandma had made them for
her. If Louise brought them to her nose now, could she smell
her mother's mother's scent? Lilies of the valley, Ivory soap,
eau de mothballs, the soft soapy powder of her ample breasts.
Was it worth the sweet and savage pain of finding out?) This
period was followed by the teen years, her high school years,
the blue jean jacket with the YES logo embroidered on the
back, Missy's vintage mouton jacket that Louise had kept
all this time out of spite, the patched blue jean skirt with
the Joni Mitchell lyrics written in indelible ink directly on
the fabric. Her history spread out before her like a fan.

Louise slipped out of her trousers. Dropping weight as
quickly as she had, she could almost fit into her old army
pants. They smelled like her, the way Louise used to smell.
Johnson's baby lotion, some faded patchouli oil, Love's
Fresh Lemon shampoo and rinse. She'd forgotten that this
scent was her scent, just like she'd forgotten a lot of things
about herself, that she could be sweet and sensitive, that

she once was easy to delight. That she could be so nuts for a guy she'd want to tear her hair out.

In her old closet, in her old house, standing on her old stepladder, Louise turned her gaze up to the two highest shelves. They were lined with various shoe boxes. She stood on tippy-toes and lifted out the one with the three letters, the dried flower, the beer bottle label, the muddy dark palette, and stepped-on smushed-up cigarette butts that had once touched his lips, all the memorabilia she had saved from their short time together, she and Scott Feinstadt. Louise lifted the shoe box off the top shelf where it sat next to a shoe box filled with *objets* from her relationship with Billy Meyers, which sat next to Rob Sacks's shoe box, and Eric Fisher's, and the three or four bulging shoe boxes, time capsules, that recorded her relationship with her ex-husband, Peter Harrington. On the next shelf up was a larger box, an old stereo box, that she absentmindedly thought of as 'miscellaneous'. In there were remnants from short affairs of the heart, finals week misadventures, her brief breakups with Peter, the smattering of one-night stands she'd had during the darkest days of her marriage. Concert ticket stubs, unused condoms (sigh), a bit of cocaine still folded in a glossy paper envelope, a squeezed-out tube of Tiger Balm, the shearing of a little gray lamb produced by an eager young poet who made her cut Peter's lab several times that spring semester and took her to the nearest field 'to see sheep' – as if seeing sheep would solve everything, which she supposed now it could. Sheep could. The sight of them.

Louise Harrington lifted out her Scott Feinstadt shoe box, with the contents she still knew by heart, but had not examined in the seventeen years since his demise, rolling around between her hands, but became so overwhelmed with fear and emotion, and fear of the emotions she might unleash by opening it (passion heartbreak angst) that she stood once again on tippy-toes and set the shoe box back down on the shelf. Her heart was racing, thunk-thump. It took a moment to catch her breath. Then she went downstairs, ate her dinner like a good girl, kissed her mother, and took the very first train she could back into town, all, miraculously, before the arrival of her brother, who liked to take dinner with his mother a couple of nights a week. *Give him the benefit of the doubt – it's not like the boy's a criminal.* Louise was in no mood for him. She would deal with Sammy later.

It was a Wednesday, the day of F. Scott Feinstadt's trumped-up interview. Louise had scheduled him at the end of the afternoon. This way she could spend the better part of the morning at Anna Sui trying to find a skirt that looked just like one she had bought at the House of Shalimar in 1981. 1981. When F. Scott Feinstadt was five years old. She finally settled on a gauzy eight-tiered swirl that flirted about her ankles. After she had paid up – a small down payment on a co-op apartment – Louise had slipped into a local coffeeshop, made her way into the bathroom and changed, shoving her jeans into the wastebasket in the corner. She looked at herself hard in the mirror – how rough her skin seemed, how large her pores were – and then took her long auburn hair – hair she had blow-dried straight for the first time in twenty years that very morning – out of its clip and fastened it in a silky loose braid. What the hell am I doing, thought Louise. Still, it was another look he'd liked.

Back at the office, F. Scott Feinstadt was late by three-quarters of an hour. Louise was prepared for this. He'd always been late before. She'd taken to telling him that the movies started a half an hour earlier than they actually began. *Midnight Express.* How hard she'd grabbed his right hand when the hero bit out his jailer's tongue. So hard, Scott Feinstadt's left hand fell from its working position on her breast.

It was five forty-eight, exactly. Louise, practically apoplectic, knew this, for she was staring at the clock when F. Scott Feinstadt knocked on her office door, which she'd left an inviting halfway open. Not easy, but available.

'Hey,' he said.

'Hey yourself,' said Louise, a little too jovially, before turning around. 'Come on in.'

She sounded like an admissions officer.

F. Scott Feinstadt came on in. He entered her office.

Louise swiveled in her chair and sized him up. He was the right height (5′10″) the right weight (155 pounds). Actually, he looked a little thicker, but he was four years older, four years older than when she'd last laid eyes upon him. His eyes were the same flawed cobalt blue (brown specks). F. Scott Feinstadt wore baggy jeans and a big, striped baggy polo shirt; his dark hair was shaved close to his pretty head. It was shaved in patterns in the back, like a basketball pro, but amongst the darker patches of his stubble, Louise could see a smattering of silver frost.

So it was him. A little older, perhaps, equipped with a set of a laugh lines. But it was him. Or some facsimile, a clone perhaps, a ghost. It was him.

It was him, now with a tattoo braceleting his wrist, crawling up his arm. When he turned to close the door behind himself, she could see two serpents, blue-and-green, inked across his neck.

It was him, but a variation.

'F.' Scott.

'It's you,' she said.

'Who?' he said, looking over his left shoulder. Then, with a little wink, he smiled at her.

That same motherfucker of a smile.

'It's you,' said Louise, gazing at him.

Back from the dead. Maybe.

Maybe not.

F. Scott Feinstadt was sitting in her office.

Louise began to talk. She heard herself reciting the entire course catalogue in a bureaucratic drone. But inside, inside! 'Hey,' she wanted to call out, 'it's me, it's me, it's me inside this grown-up body. Under the aerobicized muscles, the thickening skin, under the permanent tan line on my left ring finger, under the scars – inflicted by life, by disappointment, by my weaknesses and jealousies and flaws, inflicted by you! – it's me, it's me, your Sugar Magnolia, your Cinnamon Girl!'

She wanted to crawl across the floor, unzip his pants and suck on his cock.

Instead, she went on and on about School of the Arts course

offerings while she drank him in: 'There's "The Woman Behind the Man"; Frida Kahlo, Lee Krasner, and, for some reason I don't readily understand, Helen Frankenthaler – maybe it should just be called "The Woman"? There's "The Fallacy of the Female Form: hmmm, it says here "a cutting-edge gender study". Ah, "Figurative Drawing" . . .'

He was slow, flirty, a little shy, asking questions and then answering them himself, as had always been his way.

'You know, I'm like a rube, raised in the 'burbs, and Providence is not much of a city . . . Will I get eaten alive here? Is there any hope in the Big Apple for a small-town loser like me?' He flashed her a killer smile. Same cracked tooth up front, probably from the same skateboarding accident.

'Sure, there's hope,' he said, answering himself. He was really smiling now. 'There's always hope, right, Louise. I can tell. I can tell what you're thinking, and it's hopeful. I can read your mind.'

Louise nodded in the affirmative. Yes, F. Scott Feinstadt, she held the highest of hopes for him. Yes, he could read her mind.

At an outdoor café on Upper Broadway, they ate burritos and drank margaritas. Louise wasn't quite sure how she'd wrangled F. Scott into this 'date', but at odd moments during the evening – like when he was steering her by the elbow towards their seats when they first arrived, or when he leaned over and lit a cigarette for both of them to share after the waiter spilled their second round of drinks (she'd quit years ago, Louise said, whilst inhaling deeply; he swore he only 'partook' of tobacco when he was drinking) – Louise wasn't quite sure who exactly had been wrangling whom. That is, it had been her suggestion that they get a bite. It was late, said Louise, back at her office; she was starving and it was her professional opinion that F. Scott Feinstadt still had many unanswered questions about their program (though he'd stopped asking questions an hour or so before). Still, by the time they were seated and digging in to their black beans and sour cream and rice (her Scott Feinstadt had hated a girl on a diet, so much so that she'd stuff her face in front of him and then retire to the ladies room to puke; he'd hated a girl on a diet but he'd hated a fat girl even more) Louise had somehow felt outmaneuvered. Which was both maddening and kind of easy, actually. She'd felt some of the same powerless relief and fury she often felt on the dance floor when letting some *Strictly Ballroom*-type lead.

'So tell me, Louise Harrington,' said F. Scott, 'Why NYC? Couldn't you be doing what you're doing somewhere beautiful and cheap? Like Iowa? Couldn't you be doing what you're doing in Iowa, and ride horses or motorcycles or something and live like a queen?' He sounded a little like Jack Nicholson when he said this, as if he were making fun of every word. As if he were making fun of her. His hand swept out towards the street, indicating the sheer force and volume of the begging, amputated homeless people that had driven them to an inside table.

'Who knows,' said Louise, flustered, angry, pleased. 'I guess this is my home.'

'That's what I want,' said F. Scott, his eyes lighting up, affect lifting. 'That's what I want exactly, to have these streets as my turf.'

These streets? thought Louise. A thousand and one muffin shoppes, a thousand and one coffee bars, a million Gaps and Banana Republics. A lot of other young transplants from Larchmont, Long Island, Scarsdale. His 'turf'? In the past few years, Upper Broadway had turned into a mall. Even the burrito place where they were eating was part of a national chain. He could have had the same meal at the Cross County Shopping Center. But although it was no longer the home of De Kooning and Rauschenberg and Rothko, or even Basquiat and Haring and what's-his-name, the cracked-plate guy (the tequila was going to her head, or maybe it was, who knows?), clearly the city still turned F. Scott on. Hell, it still turned her on, when Louise bothered to think about it. The city turned on everyone who struggled to live there, it seemed, or why on earth would they bother? Louise watched as F. Scott drank all the action in: the Chinese delivery men crisscrossing on their bicycles, a bum taking a piss right in front of them, the lumbering buses, shrieking cabs, the livery cars with the naked tailpipes, the startling visible weave of all that unmitigated exhaust; and his excitement fueled her excitement, she remembered what it was like to be in the city's thrall, she remembered what it was like to be in love with it. His knees brushed against her knees. Friction. Then he moved them close by, out of range, but still present. They stayed parked half a millimeter away from Louise's knees, causing so much heat between his and hers she felt that with just a whiff of kerosene the whole world might explode.

'How about another pitcher?' said Louise. 'It's on the admissions department.' Indeed. It was on the charity of Chase Visa. Her debt. It grew like kudzu.

F. Scott shot her a drunken grin. 'Sure,' he said. 'Why not?' And then, 'Is this what they call executive recruitment?'

Did he see through her or not? It was hard to tell. It was hard to tell when he sent out such mixed signals: complete control and total naïveté. Still, he appeared to be getting progressively drunker. That, and a serenade by a crack addict in a wheelchair with an unplugged electric guitar, wailing loud enough to rouse a dog chorus, through the open café windows, was what sealed his fate. It was time to get out of there, a piece of cake bringing F. Scott back up to her apartment, with both of them already three sheets to the wind.

Ha. Louise wrangled a beautiful young boy into her apartment, one she prayed was still in possession of a pair of muscular ridges that rode the knobby track of his spine, of a hairless back, of an abdomen that she remembered came in sections. How long had it been since she'd slept with a body that didn't slide?

Louise needed this night! So she finagled F. Scott Feinstadt upstairs, pushing away the fear that her own age might prove a deterrent to the physical bliss that she was imagining so clearly now, it was a thing she could almost taste. True, buried somewhere deep in his abnormally young psyche, F. Scott Feinstadt might also remember their other life and miss her nubile image, but then again the Scott Feinstadt that she knew had been less than appreciative of her corporeal gifts. She had been so waiflike and slight back then. It had been hard, when dressed, to distinguish her breasts from her ribs. Once, after sex, Scott Feinstadt had insisted on lying on his side on his bed – his penis now a little kickstand – and examining her naked. He had Louise parade back and forth like a model – an embarrassed awkward and shy model, with hunched-over shoulders and hands that fluttered about in a weak little fan dance to hide herself. After ten agonizing minutes, Scott had declared her pretty okay – which made Louise's head feel light and her cheeks flush hot – 'if only your butt were a little higher'. Then he'd jumped up from the bed, cupped it in his hands and lifted to prove his point.

Too bad Scott Feinstadt didn't live long enough to fall victim to a slow metabolism, to a balding head and a thickening gut like the rest of the male members of their high school class (Louise had gone to her fifteenth reunion). Too bad some heartless woman somewhere didn't get to pinch his love handles and giggle, when he was striking out as an artist in New York and most needed her support. Too bad someone in as good shape as Louise was in right now didn't suggest he take up jogging while, dressed only in socks and a blue striped button-down and totally vulnerable, he was getting ready to go to work at his uncle's car dealership in Jersey.

Too bad that, unlike the rest of them, Scott Feinstadt got to die when he was perfect.

But with F. Scott Feinstadt, Louise had the home court advantage. She knew F. Scott Feinstadt would have a penchant for older women. She led him into her living room. Sat him down on the floor by the coffee table. Poured him a beer –

Scott Feinstadt had never been one to hold his liquor well. In the background, she could hear her phone ringing, the answering machine pick up: 'Wheezy, hon, it's me.' As far as Louise was concerned, Missy could go fuck herself. Had she ever deigned to pick up the phone when Louise had called when Missy had had Scott Feinstadt over? No. Of course not. Missy had let the damned thing ring and ring, even when she knew Louise had seen them enter the house together, even when she knew Louise knew that she and Scott Feinstadt were home alone, even when she knew Louise knew Missy's mother was out of town. 'Is something up with you?' asked Missy now, her nasal Larchmont lockjaw polluting Louise's airwaves, clogging up her home. 'My vibe thing's telling me there's something up with you. And you were such a total weirdo earlier on the phone . . .' Fuck her. Fuck Missy and her vibe thing. Nosy fucking bitch. I'm not letting you anywhere near this one. Louise turned her attentions back to F. Scott.

'Peanuts?' she said. 'Cheese?'

'I'm fine,' he said. 'I'm perfect.' He smiled at her. Appreciatively. Like it was possible that he found her pretty. He didn't look like he thought she was too old for him. She remembered Scott Feinstadt telling her this himself, about the 'old lady fetish', as he called it, when they were lying naked in Manor Park one night twenty-one years before on a blanket made up of their cutoff shorts and black concert T-shirts, her lacy white bra curled like a kitten at his ankles.

It was post-facto, and over before she knew it, and she was antsy and he was spent, and they were lying a foot apart and not-touching on the hot moist lawn that led up to the little local beach, a tiny pathetic spit of sand

– his words punctuated by the obscene, wet slap of the Sound.

In order to get a conversation going – it was embarrassing, lying apart and naked like that, her thighs squid-white in the moonlight; it was embarrassing, to have been as dry as a desert and not having come and not having the time to have properly faked it – Louise was bemoaning the fact that she was getting older. A senior in high school. Used goods. When so many pretty skinny little freshman girls were dying to take her place.

She reached out her hand to his.

She didn't want to lose him. No matter how self-centered he was, no matter that he was a lousy lover. She was seventeen. What did she know but lousy lovers? None of that mattered, not the strange pungent mix of his 'natural' deodorant and his body odor, his silly affectations, his incredible self-love.

'Not to worry,' said Scott Feinstadt. 'I really dig older women. I mean really old, like thirty-four or thirty-five. As long as they're still in shape. Strong girls. That's when they're at their sexual height. For a guy, it's nineteen. So you're lucky. You're catching me at my peak.'

Then he rolled over and mounted her again.

Lucky? thought Louise. Moments before you were hanging over me like a panting dog, tongue stuck between your teeth. Now you're hot and squishy against my chest. Will any of this make you love me?

But in her apartment, as an adult, making out on her floor, on a bunch of velvet Moroccan pillows, harem-style, with an older but still young F. Scott Feinstadt, Louise changed her tune. I'm lucky, she thought, I'm so very lucky to be here now with him. For it seemed like in the four intervening years – four years F. Scott Feinstadt time – he had picked up some pointers. He was passionate, kissing up and down her neck. He was passionate worrying at her earlobe. His body was familiar. So boyish and so beautiful. When he pulled his shirt off over the back of his head, his once hairless chest now sported curly black spirals around the nipples, and further down in the bottom quadrants of his stomach, it got curlier and thicker still, leading a woolly path to his groin.

Who is this guy? Louise thought. What the hell am I doing here with him? Am I completely crazy? Am I pathetic? A pedophile? A deviant? And then, she thought, I can't believe how lucky I am. To have a second chance.

The phone rang again. The machine picked up. It was Peter.

'Lou,' he said. 'It's me. I had my meeting today with Sammy. Pretty damn interesting. You've heard, I trust, of DVDs . . .'

'Wait a minute,' said F. Scott. 'Don't you want to talk?'

Talk? To Peter? She could talk to Peter anytime.

'Oh, God no,' said Louise. 'It's just Peter, my ex-husband.'

'An ex-husband,' said F. Scott. 'Sexy.'

The answering machine cut Peter off. The phone immediately began to ring again. Louise resumed kissing F. Scott, hands caressing his face, his ears, hoping her open palms pressed flatly against the side of his head just might muffle the sound.

'Listen, I took the liberty of buying you a new answering machine,' said Peter. 'One that doesn't instantly cut the speaker o . . .' Click.

F. Scott pulled away again.

'No, I'm serious, Louise,' said F. Scott, sounding, well, serious. 'I want to talk. You and I, we have a chance, we have a chance at having really good sex, because I'm open to you, you know? And I hope, I'm really hoping that you'll be open to me . . . so I want to know more about you. I've rushed things before, and it was a mistake. I don't want to make mistakes with you. I want to know as much as I can about you before we make love.' Here he reached out his hand, he was shy about it, like he was offering himself to her, like he was risking something, but also like he was confidant, confidant that for once he was handling something right. He took her hand in his beautiful dry palm with the dark, inky remnants of his paints creasing his love line and his life line – so achingly short, she thought, unless that was just the pigment thinning out? – like a fine etching.

'Make love?'

When was the last time anyone had seduced her just by putting her off?

Scott Feinstadt. He'd done the same thing their first time in the back of his truck. He'd got her going, first with his fingers on the outside of her panties, and then he'd slipped them inside, inside the panties, oh, and then into her. Then he put his mouth down there until she was crazy, his tongue so strong and warm, and then out of nowhere, just when her head was about to spin off her neck, just when she was sure she was losing it, he'd stopped short. He removed himself, so that Louise was so loose and trembly she felt that if someone were to pull a secret thread she would have unraveled and fallen apart. He'd stopped her, because he was the sensitive one, and she the overeager anxious slut. He'd stopped her, even though he'd done it with Berta and Trisha and Theresa Longo and probably half of Rome, while this was Louise's first anything. The experienced Scott Feinstadt had Louise Silverstein, the virgin, begging for it.

'I want to wait until it's right,' said Scott Feinstadt.

'I want to wait until I'm sure.'

Then Mr Sandra Dee Feinstadt drove her home, Louise as limp as a noodle, but somehow still fidgety, like a partially downed telephone wire, its open end still shooting an occasional spark but curling weakly against the grass. Louise was pressed up miserably against the truck door on her side of the front seat, embarrassed and ashamed, while Scott Feinstadt sang along softly with the radio, Springsteen's 'Born to Run', once in a while deigning to pat her knee, his eyes locked on the road ahead of him. She was so afraid that night, afraid that she'd turned him off, afraid that she was, as Missy had proclaimed Berta to be, 'too sexual', afraid that she'd never get a second chance.

Now she was older, wiser.

'Okay, F. Scott,' she said. 'Let's talk.'

F. Scott combed his fingers through her fingers. 'Your hands are so beautiful, they look like Georgia O'Keeffe's. Are you an artist?'

'No,' said Louise. 'I'm the School of the Arts acting admissions coordinator.'

'I think I know that, already,' he smiled at her shyly. 'But what are you in your heart?'

In her heart, that wobbly, faltering muscle, that generator of panic and fear? What was she in her heart but lonely?

'I don't know,' said Louise softly. She hated him.

F. Scott Feinstadt's right index finger grazed across her collarbone.

'Maybe I can help you figure it out,' he said.

She didn't have time for this. Anything could happen now. They could be struck by lightning, her university housing could burn down, she could have a stroke. Peter might call back. Terrorists could attack. She could die, he could die, anyone could die before they did 'it'.

It had been known to happen. People had died before.

When she was younger, when he was younger, there were hours and hours for this kind of Scott Feinstadt talk. He wanted fame, he wanted immortality. He thought his paintings would enter the canon, and Louise had believed him then, listening to him with awe. He was so much, well, fuller, than she was. Oh sure, she was a good student, a better student than Scott Feinstadt, and she was certainly pretty enough, but she'd always lacked a burning desire to be specific in the world. Even at nineteen, Scott Feinstadt was specific in the world. 'I don't want a just-add-water life,' said Scott. This impressed her. Captivated her, even. In a wounded spaceship spiraling off course – which was often how she saw her life as it was suspended in the gravity-free chamber of adolescence – she would have given him her share of oxygen readily if she could. Peter was specific in the world. For a while, she'd been content spinning in his orbit. Now who cared about specificity, or anybody's orbit. All she sought was a little pleasure. She'd keep her oxygen for herself, thank you. Is that what it meant to finally grow up?

F. Scott Feinstadt was going on. See, his parents were

willing to spring for his tuition. He knew he should probably just move out to Williamsburg, get a day job and paint his ass off, but he'd never really been out of school before, and he guessed – his finger exploring the hollows above her breasts – he was a little scared. Of the real world.

Oh, God, thought Louise. I'm not seventeen anymore. I don't have to listen to this.

She decided to take matters into her own hands.

Literally.

'On second thought,' said F. Scott Feinstadt, smiling, 'There's a lot of different ways to get to know each other. Far be it from me to rank one higher than the other.'

Had he purposely pushed her to this point?

In a minute they were both naked, off the pillows and on the floor, the coffee table shoved into a corner, existential crises now mercifully forgotten.

He stopped for just a moment to pull his wallet out of his jeans. He plucked out a condom, a fluorescent yellow lubricated Sheik, and said: 'Is this all right? I mean I want to be certain that you're not doing anything you didn't want to.'

That same old Scott Feinstadt line.

'It's fine,' said Louise. 'It's good.' And when he fumbled a little with the rubber, she said under her breath: 'Come on.'

Once cloaked, F. Scott Feinstadt stuck out in front of himself like a luminous yellow wand.

The phone rang again.

'It's Mom.'

'I guess you're pretty popular,' said F. Scott.

He rolled on top of her, with her mother yammering away in the background.

'I ran into Fran Horowitz this afternoon – you know she's still chief fundraiser for the synagogue, although how, when everybody hates her, who knows? Anyway, I told her you were asking about the Feinstadts and she's been e-mailing with Rachel – what's e-mail anyway, I mean, really? Isn't it just another way for the FBI to keep track?'

'Feinstadt?' said F. Scott.

In a panic, Louise turned the tables and she rolled on top of him, his dick almost slipping out on her way up, but saved by a firm wresting of her position with her thighs.

'Mmm,' said F. Scott Feinstadt, 'whatever the hell you want.'

At that point, thankfully, Mom was cut off.

Who was this guy, this cute young guy, this MFA applicant that Louise was fucking?

And what did it matter, now that she was finally getting a piece of what she wanted? Now Louise was on top. She was on top and liking it. This F. Scott Feinstadt had melted into a blissful and helpless puddle between her hips. Every few seconds or so he would arch up, or thrust or twitch or something, a little weak smile teasing at his lips, but at best his rhythm was syncopated and close to annoying, so soon, through caresses and a careful squeezing of her inner muscles, Louise seized control of the situation, F. Scott Feinstadt giving up.

When they were young, Louise and Scott Feinstadt, the summer nights in Larchmont were thick with the scent of pollen and perfume, the smell of gasoline, of pot, of cigarettes, of bug spray and his deodorant. Their young naked bodies were softened by the filmy haze of suburban starlight; they were as blurry and unreal as if a cinematographer were viewing them through a layer of shimmery gauze. When they were young, Louise would spread her legs and let Scott Feinstadt enter her, whether she was ready or not, whether it hurt her or not, and she'd murmur encouraging words to him, 'Oh baby, oh Scott,' or perhaps just little humming sounds or little squelched yelps when he'd push too far. She'd stroke his long thin back, his smooth skin with the little smattering of zit bumps, from his bony shoulders down to the dimples in his butt, as he pumped and pumped, rubbing her raw, hurting her. She'd lie beneath him as sweat dripped off his chin and nose, sweat slapped from his chest to her chest, his eyes closed, his head thrown back, mouth open. He'd looked like a wheezing bulldog.

Now it was Louise who was sweating, Louise who was doing all the work. F. Scott Feinstadt wriggled weakly beneath her weight. This time he would get the rug burn and her perspiration would coat his bare skin like misty rain. Louise glanced down. His lips were parted, in the corner was a little pearl of drool. Although he sported a five o'clock shadow, the skin beneath the tiny dark scratches of beard appeared smooth. His hairline seemed to recede just a bit further back than she remembered it, as if it were only at low tide.

When they were young, Louise used to talk, she talked a lot while they were making love. All the books said to do this, all the books she perused while baby-sitting, after scouring the medicine cabinets for Valiums and Percodans, after smoking all of her neighbors' pot. Louise would read their sex books and then take back what she'd learned to Scott. She'd say: 'Show me what you like, Sweetheart.' She would communicate, because after all, communication was what the sex books all said good sex was all about. So as he pumped in and out, Louise would say: 'I love you, Scott; I love you, honey,' in intervals of about seventy-five seconds. She counted. She counted the intervals between her words of encouragement and the moments until it was over. Then she'd lie there – on the bed, in the car, on the lawn – thinking, soon it'll be over, soon it'll be over, and it was never ever over; sometimes it felt like his fucking her went on forever (since that first time he'd stopped bothering with a warmup); then other times it was over before she knew it.

But when it was over, when he had come, when he had finished, he would completely collapse, sinking down on Louise, his hipbones grinding into her pelvis, the weight of his body flattening out her lungs, making it hard to breathe, the soft tender tissue of her vagina aflame and burning so much so that after a couple of rounds of this maybe there would be blood; and certainly when she peed, even in the shower, it would sting.

Now, in her apartment with F. Scott Feinstadt, it was Louise who was keeping it going, getting him to the brink, then pulling back, then getting him to the brink again. The poor kid was all shiver and moan.

He said, 'You're killing me, you're killing me. Kill me,' he said. 'Please.'

So with a slow in and out she pleased him.

Only when he was done did she finally allow herself to come. They slid away from one another in a loose knot, on her living room floor, F. Scott Feinstadt's right arm slung haphazardly across her waist as he lightly, lightly began to snore, while Louise tried to even out her own breathing, to calm her racing heart.

When they were young, after it was over, Louise would lie naked on the naked earth with the full weight of a totaled Scott Feinstadt on top of her, smothering her, crushing her, driving her hard into the ground. She'd think, someday I will find someone who loves me, someday I'll get married and have a husband, someday sex will be something I like, it will be something good.

Now she was lying half-clothed – for she still had on her T-shirt – on her floor with a boy half her age, dead asleep, in her arms. His mouth was open and a little spit bubble breathed in and out of the corner. She smelled his buzzed head; it was sweaty and sweet as a baby's. What had she done? She could lose her job for this. Now that he'd slept with her, maybe this strange kid thought he could gain admission to the graduate program of his choice. Or worse yet, maybe he might fall in love.

She wriggled out from under his arm. She covered him with one of her sofa throws. Then she got up and went into the kitchen, looking for a cigarette. In the cookie jar was her emergency pack. She tapped one out and lit up. Smoking, she went back into the living room. A beautiful naked boy was sleeping on her rug.

She'd fucked him.

When they were young, when they were done, Louise would trace the words 'I love you' across Scott Feinstadt's still panting moist back with the tip of her right forefinger, employing the same hope and delicacy with which she might have traced those same heartfelt words on a steamed-up back-seat window. She'd say: 'That was great, Scott, I really love you,' which was true, the second part was true, she really loved him; she loved him and she loved him and she loved him, and she was never going to get over him, no matter what anybody had to say about puppy love and life experience; no, Louise never was going to get over the stupid dead boy she loved with all her heart when she was so ridiculously improbably young that it should have been against the law.

It should have been against the law to be as young as Louise once was.

And now, at last, she was old.

The phone rang.

'It's your mother. Anybody home?'

No, thought Louise. No, Mom. Lights out. Nobody's home.

———◆———

When she woke up in the morning, Louise hoped it had all been a dream, the seduction, the sex, the doppelgänger weirdo stuff, but it wasn't. Not a moment of it. Clearly none of it had been a dream at all. She was T-shirted and pantyless and sticky, and lying half-covered by his blue jean jacket on her floor. F. Scott Feinstadt's blue jean jacket, with the dirty rolled-up cuffs. The floor was dirty, too. She could get an infection. Crumbs and paint speckles – oils or acrylics? had they flecked themselves off his sneaks? – clung to her bare bottom. She tried to slap them off. This wasn't a dream. A used condom sat in a limp gooky little pile by the coffee table, a fly lazing in its juices. This was a Bunuel film. This was her life. No dreams. No dreams around for miles. So Louise hoped for the next best thing. She hoped for a one-night stand. She hoped for a boy who would 'do' her and use her, and silently slip out her front door before morning. She hoped for Scott Feinstadt, back from the dead, heartless and headstrong and riddled with all those conflicting masculine traits that she could only think of as 'boy disease'.

Instead, she found F. Scott.

In her kitchen, making breakfast. He was making break-fast. For her. Raisin pancakes, with homemade raisin syrup – a box of brown sugar and a bottle of rum were sitting on her counter.

'Good morning,' said F. Scott, smiling. He handed her a mug of coffee. One of her towels was slung around his waist. He'd already showered. He smiled again, or was it mere continuation? 'I hope you don't mind,' he said, 'I made myself at home with your toothbrush.'

Mind? Why should she mind? She'd kissed him enough last night to share a lifetime's worth of communicable diseases.

Louise sipped at her coffee. It was surprisingly good. Her eyes roamed the kitchen counter. He'd ferreted out her coffee grinder and the old Sicilian espresso maker. It looked like he'd even warmed up some steamed milk.

'Mmmm,' said Louise, because it was the only thing she could think of to say that was true.

'The pancakes should be ready in a few minutes,' said

F. Scott. 'Why don't you take your shower while I pour your juice?'

Why not indeed? Louise nodded in the affirmative. A shower and strong coffee. Maybe one or the other would startle her back into gear. She headed towards the bathroom.

'Wait,' said F. Scott. 'Need this?' and he went to whip off his towel, from the corner of his waist, where it hung so fetchingly near to his hipbone. 'It was the only one that I could find.' That's because all the rest are neatly folded in the linen closet, you boy!, she felt like shouting in his ear. Instead, her eye caught sight of a blue-green rose twining out of the curly black forest of his pubic hair. My God, thought Louise, is that another tattoo? But no, it looked like a love bite. Was that Louise's doing?

Help me, she thought, someone. Peter? Mom?

'That's okay,' she said. 'Keep it on.' Who wanted to know? She made a point of going to the linen closet, and taking out a pile of carefully folded matching towels, bath, body, and facecloth, all in the same velvety green hue. I bet the last time you saw things this organized, she thought, was at home in the suburbs with your own mother.

In the steam of her shower, the scented votives lit – F. Scott had lit them – the world softened in a perfumed haze. Perhaps, she thought, none of this was as bad as she'd first surmised. So what, she'd had her fun with an applicant half her age?

Who would ever know? Even if he brought it to the dean's attention, it would only amount to a he said, she said, wouldn't it? Louise made a mental note to check F. Scott's blue jean jacket for evidence.

She took her time toweling off and then she luxuriated in her daily application of body cream. Slathered her face and throat. Picked over her eyebrows with a tweezers. Mascara. An eyelash curler. Lipstick and blush. She even pushed back her cuticles on her hands and toes with an orange stick. Anything to place her best foot forward, anything to delay her reemergence. Anything not just to face him, but to face him with pride. Then, at last, when there were no more beauty products left to make use of, she turbaned her head and wrapped herself safely in the bath towel, inhaled a deep breath and took the plunge. She opened the bathroom door.

'Soup's on,' said F. Scott, calling from the living room. 'But take your time; I took the liberty of laying out your clothes.'

'Took the liberty'? What? Huh? Louise made her way from the bathroom down the hall to her bedroom with her eyes shut. Once safely in her room, she opened them. There on her bed were a pair of black jeans and a silky blouse. Suitable enough for work. Underwear and bra. The lacy stuff. What had been buried deep down in her dresser drawer. Never been worn. *There had never been a need to wear them.* She didn't know whether or not to feel violated. She didn't know whether or not to feel touched.

Obediently, Louise donned her laid-out outfit. She brushed her hair back into a ponytail. While she was finishing her toilette, she laid out her master plan: to let him down gently. 'It was nice, *F.*,' she planned to say, 'but ...' We're too mismatched, etc., etc., maybe I taught you something about sex, maybe we're both a little better for it ... Now toddle on home to the twenty-year-old girl of your dreams.

'Hey, Louise Harrington,' called F. Scott, piercing her reverie.

'What F. Scott,' Louise called back out to him.

'I can't find the cat dish.'

The cat dish? What cat dish? Was this some new form of sexual slang?

'What cat dish?' Louise again called out to him.

'You know, for the cat,' said F. Scott. 'I figured as long as I was making breakfast, I'd make a special treat for him.'

'I don't have a cat,' said Louise, under her breath.

'The cat dish,' said F. Scott, repeating himself. 'I can't hear you.'

What the fuck was he talking about? She glanced at her clock. Nine-thirty. She never got into the office later than 10:00. A perfect excuse to hightail it out of there. Instead, she picked up the phone to call and make her apologies – the nonexistent cat was sick, the alarm hadn't gone off (what alarm? she got up every morning at six like a farmer, a leftover from all those years of bedding down with Peter, the self-described country boy), she had a doctor's appointment; but then she realized there was no one for her to call. She was the acting admissions coordinator. She was the one in charge. Meekly, she padded out of her bedroom. F. Scott had also taken the liberty of laying out her socks.

'Look,' he said, holding up a frying pan, in the kitchen.

'Fried chicken livers. I found some frozen in your freezer.'
He laughed. 'Can you say it ten times fast?'

Fried chicken livers frozen in your freezer, fried chicken livers frozen in your freezer, fried chicken livers . . .

'I don't have a cat,' said Louise.

'You don't?'

'I don't.'

'Wow, I thought girls like you always had a cat,' said F. Scott, putting down the pan.

He was dressed and sipping from his cup of joe and he followed her into the living room. The coffee table was set. One of her bonsais sat in the middle of it like a centerpiece. He looked up from his mug and smiled.

Because she didn't know what to say, Louise just stood where she was and licked her lips.

'Baby,' said F. Scott. 'Come here and say that.'

Come here and say that. Her heart fell below her belt. It beat there.

Again, Louise obeyed him. She walked towards him as if in a trance. When she arrived inside the confines of his personal space, he reached out, reeled her in with one hand and then the other, and then F. Scott kissed her. But good.

'I don't have a goddamn cat,' Louise said. She said it coldly, although she was still blinking from the kiss.

She thought she saw him wince.

They sat down at the coffee table, on the floor again, across from one another. He'd made her breakfast. His eyes were wide. She felt guilty for having snapped at him.

'They look good,' said Louise. 'The pancakes.'

They did, round and golden.

'It's the only thing I know I'm good at,' F. Scott said, she thought, a tad suggestively. Was he fishing for compliments? Or being sincere? It was hard to tell with him.

It had been hard to tell with the other one.

'Why don't you dive right in?'

Why not? Louise picked up her fork and took the plunge. Buttery. Where had he found butter in her household? Even the syrup was good. It reminded her of her youth.

At Missy's, after a sleepover, or late at night when they were stricken with the munchies, they'd break out the frozen waffles and head straight for the brown sugar.

Frozen food?

Mom had only fed her kids the fresh stuff.

It was quiet for a while while Louise dug in, too quickly to bother tallying calories, to pay attention to the voices inside her head – was she a schizophrenic? Who cared, the pancakes were that good.

'Well,' said Louise, between bites. She hadn't realized she had been quite so ravenous. 'Well.'

'Well, what, sweetie?' said F. Scott, smiling. Half her plate was emptied, but she noticed he hadn't even taken one bite of his. Typical. Typical of him. *Mr Manipulator.*

'Well, I'm late for work,' said Louise, suddenly standing up. 'You can let yourself out, the door locks automatically.'

'Does it?' said F. Scott, still seated.

'Yes,' said Louise. 'It does.'

She flustered around the room a little, grabbing a jacket, her purse, checking for her wallet and her keys. A lipstick. Then she headed for the door, aware always of his eyes on her, but never daring to meet them.

She was the same as she ever was.

(Shy.)

Only different.

For example, now she sounded like a steely-spined flight attendant. 'Well, have a good day,' she said, in a clipped, professional way, oddly chirpy; have a good day! with her fingers on the door knob. As the door was halfway open, Louise looked up straight at him – F. Scott was grinning that stupid grin, and then, according to plan (or actually, in spite of it): 'You won't tell anyone about this, will you?' She averted her gaze again. 'I mean I'm a lot older than you are.'

In an instant, he was right behind her, his arms around her waist, beneath her ribs, in that way she'd always loved a boy to hold her.

'Louise Harrington, Acting Admissions Coordinator, it was great being with you last night. In fact, I loved being with you last night.'

He kissed the back of her neck. Softly. His lips were just the tiniest bit chapped. Probably from all that kissing. They tickled her.

'I'm not ashamed of anything.'

Wow, she thought. That's nice.

'I mean anything having to do with you.' He chuckled. A little revolted shiver rippled up her spine.

F. Scott gave her another squeeze when he felt her stiffen. Then he whispered.

'I'm happy, Louise. Aren't you?'

He turned her around, looked into her eyes with his eyes, Scott Feinstadt's eyes, the same cobalt blue, brown specks, although F. Scott's left eye seemed to have its own peculiar flaw in the iris, a little extended coffee-colored island. 'I'm not exactly jailbait you know. You're not that much older than me.'

'Oh yeah,' she said.

'Not in your soul,' said F. Scott, wisely.

The soul business. It was so queer. But could it also be true? It was what she wanted, to be young in her soul, when her exterior was so polished, so hard now, when the skin around her eyes was as lined as a long-ago etching of her face Scott Feinstadt had scratched out on a napkin he'd moments earlier used to wipe his mouth. 'Here,' Scott Feinstadt had said, pushing the napkin across the Formica tabletop, careful to skirt it around a little blob of spilt ketchup at the McDonald's on White Plains Road, 'take a look at yourself.' Louise had looked then at the big brown eyes, the babyish round cheeks, small chin, the half-smile that played around the lips of what at that time had made up her image, and all she'd seen were the multitudinous lines he'd used to form her, as if he'd fashioned her out of a spider's web. 'I look so old,' said Louise; in fact she'd blurted it; she was that disappointed. Scott Feinstadt laughed out loud. 'It's not your actual face, sweetie,' he said. 'It's your true face,' said Scott Feinstadt. 'You have quite an old soul, Wheezy.' Wheezy. He must have already begun sleeping with Missy, behind her back. Wow. She'd never realized that before. For a moment, she felt angry and hurt all over again; she felt like killing her, Missy; incongruously, she even felt like giving F. Scott Feinstadt's face a smack. But she restrained herself. Sins of the father, right? Sins of the reincarnated other? Sins of a bastard that some sinless kid just happened to resemble?

But at the time, back in their youth, Louise was still innocent of Missy's betrayal. She was still innocent and still willing to study Scott Feinstadt's every word. An old soul. She hadn't known then whether or not to take that comment as a compliment, and so she'd tried her best to be giddy and gay the rest of the afternoon, she'd tried her best not to be so serious, to be young, until around four-fifteen when Scott Feinstadt had looked at his watch – he was working the late shift – and told her not to try so hard, what he liked about her was that she usually didn't give him such a headache. Now, about a million years later, her eyes locked with the flawed but beautiful eyes of young F. Scott Feinstadt, she felt a deep and residing connection.

Did he feel it too?

Louise felt her arms and legs fill with liquid light. She closed her eyes again, waiting to be kissed.

But there was no kiss. *Stupid girl.* Of course no kiss, only a quick pat on her butt and then F. Scott Feinstadt pushed her out into the hallway. 'Have a good day,' he said. Was his tone genuine or mocking? Have a good day. And then, 'A cat might keep you company.' With that, Louise's mysterious houseguest shut her door behind her.

Alone, angry, confused, excited, the love pat still burning on her backside, Louise thought, who am I trying to kid?

She'd met her match. Again.

'I hate cats,' said Louise, although there was no one living or dead in that empty vestibule to hear.

It was hard to get anything done, back at Columbia in her little office, knowing that F. Scott Feinstadt was on his own in her apartment, free to roam. It was hard to sit quietly at her desk. First of all, she was still tender. That is, Louise couldn't find a comfortable position in which to sit. She hoped the shenanigans of the previous night would not bring on a case of 'honeymoon' cystitis; it had been a long time since Louise had kept a bottle of cranberry juice in her fridge. That's what she remembered best about her freshman-year dorm, the growing exhibition, as the semester progressed, of cranberry juice bottles on display in the communal refrigerator – each affixed with a lucky girl's name markered on a strip of masking tape; that, and the hall bathroom (with the door that actually locked) that always faintly smelt of vomit. What good was a lock to her now that a boy was alone in her apartment?

Suddenly, Louise understood why Missy had insisted on videotaping the nanny, behind the nanny's back, while Missy was out of the house. She'd made Marcos drag out all his fancy directing equipment, and the two of them had viewed the tape in bed in the evening over popcorn (with salt and butter, no more air-popping for Missy) while the unsuspecting star ate her rice and beans and watched *Wheel of Fortune* in the kitchen. (Missy had a TV in almost every room of her house. In the master bath she

had one. 'Like at the Four Seasons,' said Missy.) The tape
had proved fairly boring, as boring as spending a day alone
with the kids, said Missy wryly.

What she wouldn't give now for Marcos and his fancy
directing equipment. What was F. Scott doing in her home?
How could she have left him there, a veritable stranger?
For all she knew, at this very moment, he was lugging out
a pillowcase stuffed full of her wedding silver.

'I don't need a fucking cat,' said Louise aloud in her office.
'I have plenty of fucking company.' Peter, I have Peter.

Louise decided to pick up the phone. She thought she was
dialing Peter but somehow she ended up calling herself; her
fingers did the dialing. She waited for her voice to spring up
on the answering tape. She could leave a message. See how
everything was going. But no outgoing recording bothered to
click on. The phone rang and rang. It rang endlessly. Perhaps
he'd also stolen the answering machine. It would be a small
price to pay for her transgressions. She almost welcomed the
thought, F. Scott Feinstadt ripping off virtually everything,
Louise coming home to an apartment stripped bare, wiped
nice and clean of her artifacts, of any telltale signs of her
history. It would give her the opportunity to begin her
life anew again. Or, maybe the answering machine was
just plain full. Certainly, it seemed as if anyone who had
ever called her before had bothered to pick up the horn
last night.

Is that what had happened to her the previous evening?
She'd been so full she'd stopped recording much. Because
hard as Louise tried, it wasn't easy to remember specif-
ics, like how he'd gotten that love bite on his hip, for

example. All she could legitimately conjure was the sensation of being so swept away by revenge, by anger and bitterness, by the sheer heady pleasure of sex, sex with someone young and beautiful, not terribly experienced but beautiful just the same. All she could remember was being alive.

Louise hung up. She turned to the application in her lap. She turned to the application on her desk. She stood and turned to the applications that lined her windowsill. She sat back down with application number one again. I'm not going to do it this time, she thought, waste my days like a lovesick puppy. I'm smarter than that now. I'm not going to moon.

The phone rang.

She picked up. 'Louise Harrington, Acting Admissions Coordinator.'

'F. Scott Feinstadt,' he said. 'Star-six-nine.'

He'd had the phone company retrieve her call.

'Oh,' she said, adjusting her hips to a more comfortable position in her seat. 'How are you?'

'Lonely,' he said. 'You?'

'Lonely,' she said.

Was something leaking out of her underwear? Hadn't he been wearing a condom? Had it broken? She thought, don't think about it. She thought, for once in your life, don't care.

'I saw the painting in your living room.'

Louise's heart stopped. Thunk-thump. Flutter, flutter. Instinctively, her hand reached for the emergency pack of cigarettes in her desk.

'I liked it. Although I found it a little naive, you know? A little retro. It looked like something I might have done in my youth.'

She lit up. Inhaled. Her heart fluttered.

'How about dinner tomorrow night?'

'How about it,' she said.

Boy was she clever.

'We could go to an art opening. Get some free wine and cheese.'

'We could,' said Louise, thinking, I guess I picked myself another live one, free wine and cheese. Classy.

'We will,' said F. Scott. 'I'll call for you at eight. Now I've got to motor or I'm going to miss my train. You wouldn't happen to have a schedule?'

'To Larchmont?' Louise squeaked out. 'I mean, Mamaroneck?'

'Why would I want to go there?'

There was silence on the line.

'Your post office box,' said Louise. 'I mean, I just figured . . .'

'I live on Long Island, Louise,' F. Scott Feinstadt said, 'when I'm not crashing with some buddies up in Providence. My old roommate from art school set up the post office box for me in Larchmont, just to keep my parents off my scent. You know, grad school, Columbia. All that ivy. It would make my dad so happy to know I'd applied, he'd probably have a stroke.'

'Why didn't you just use one of those mailbox places?' said Louise, suspiciously.

'Hey,' said F. Scott Feinstadt, slowly. 'Because that would have been smart . . .'

'Ms Cipriani?' Louise croaked out. She felt like she was about to cry.

'She was my counselor up at camp. I dated her daughter. Behind her back. I ran into her one weekend when I was visiting my old roommate up in Westchester.'

'When?' said Louise, she could barely catch her breath. Ms Cipriani's daughter? Who even knew she had one? Who even knew she had a life outside of Mamaroneck High School's hallowed halls?

'Until about six o'clock last night.'

What, thought Louise. Until me?

'Now don't cry,' he said.

'I'm not, I'm choking,' said Louise.

'Then don't choke, cause I don't have the time to run over there and resuscitate you. I forgot to call home last night and if I get back in time I can pretend to have written my mom a note saying I was staying at Ricky's and that the note fell behind the stove . . .'

'Ricky?'

'My buddy. I always tell my mom I'm staying with Ricky when I'm staying with some girl.'

'Some girl?'

'Relax, Louise. You're different. You know you're different. I don't have to tell you that, because you know it all ready. But Mom, she worries . . .'

'Wouldn't want that,' said Louise. 'Wouldn't want Mom to worry.'

'No,' said F. Scott. 'My mom's great.'

And the phone went dead.

I'm fucking a twenty-four-year-old who's got a crush on his

mother, thought Louise. I'm fucking a twenty-four-year-old who fucked Ms Cipriani's daughter. At least Scott Feinstadt had never stooped so low . . . although Ms Cipriani's daughter had probably just been a glimmer in Ms Cipriani's eye back then. If the kid had been old enough to flirt back, well, nothing would have stopped Scott Feinstadt.

Louise had to rest her head. She lay it down on her desk on a pillow of applications. Resting it that way, she did her best to quietly hyperventilate, wondering if enough oxygen was really reaching her brain.

Still, Louise felt perkier. He'd called. They'd have a second date. With the original Scott Feinstadt, she'd had to ask. Breathing heavily, Louise could still remember that singular humiliation. 'Um, Scott, are we going to see each other again, or was this just a one-night stand?' A one-night stand, when all they'd done was make out on the loading dock behind Cheese Bazaar among the prosciutto scraps and the wine-washed cheese rinds. The original Scott Feinstadt had only furthered her humiliation. 'It's two o'clock in the afternoon, Louise,' he'd said. 'God, you're cute. You know that?'

'What an idiot you are,' said Missy helpfully, when for the first and last time, Louise relayed point by point the day's activities with Scott Feinstadt to her best friend as the two of them got stoned that evening in the woods behind Missy's house. 'What a social reject,' said Missy. But by the time Louise had stumbled her way home later that same night, there was a message scrawled on the notepad by the phone stand in her kitchen. Mom had written it. It read: 'The rabbi's son has deigned to call. Don't go getting religious on us, honey.' Had there been no end to the embarrassments

Louise endured? Still, at the time she'd thought, fuck you, Missy. She'd thought: Missy, zero. Louise, one.

But now things were entirely different. Louise had only had to wonder if she would hear from F. Scott Feinstadt again for about an hour. *And fifteen minutes; don't pretend you didn't count.* Shut up! Louise screamed inside her head. She'd finally caught her breath. Feeling newly empowered and invigorated, she gave herself permission to say it aloud. 'Shut up, Mom,' said Louise, inside her new office. Thus released, the tension leaking its way out of the tips of her manicured fingers, she went back to her work with renewed vigor, on the hunt, combing her pile for automatic rejects. She turned to her computer and called up the university's standard ding letter. 'We're sorry to say . . . *Ding!*' In the past, this was one of the tasks that Louise hadn't minded, a little mailmerge, a trip downstairs to the coffee bar, saving the applicant a large fortune in tuition bills, preventing them from mortgaging their future. Ding, ding, ding. But now she was in the mood to say yes to life. She studied the form, and added a new and hopeful line: 'We encourage you to reapply.' One never knew what could happen in the future.

After work, Louise stopped back at her apartment. She flung the door wide open, half-hoping to find F. Scott still lounging in her towel. Instead, she was met by a blast of cool sweet air. It was a particularly warm spring day and he'd left on the air-conditioning. What did he care, it's not like he knew from electric bills, it's not like he was old enough to have to pay his own way, to take some fiscal responsibility for anything himself. Mr Perpetual Student. But a half-smile found its way onto Louise's face. There had been an afternoon that fateful summer. Scott Feinstadt's parents were away in the Poconos for the weekend. The temperature had topped off at 99 degrees, *but with the humidity, it must have been one hundred and three. One hundred and three?* Why not one hundred and five or ten? *Three? Three! What do you remember?* Louise remembered. She and Scott Feinstadt had been having sex all afternoon in the Feinstadt's living room with the air-conditioning on full blast. Even with the workout he was giving her, Louise had felt the chill. Her thighs, freshly shaved, were covered with goosebumps, her skin looked yellowy blue – 'like a chicken breast at the IGA,' Scott Feinstadt said, romantically. How his words stung her. Why, even to this day, the skin on her thighs in cold weather looked to her like some prized product of Frank Perdue's. A tear had slipped out of Louise's eye back then, no matter that she'd been blinking them back with the frequency of a geisha with a fan.

'Hey,' said Scott Feinstadt. 'Don't cry. We can turn up the heat.'

Oh God, Louise thought. Please. Please don't make him want to have sex again. Because already her vulva suffered a steady burn – she'd treat it later with a gingered application of Vaseline, cursing all those condoms without lubricants, those motherfucking Sheiks – Louise couldn't will herself through another round. But Scott Feinstadt was hopping to his feet. Naked, his high, proud balls giving a little swing, he made his way over to the fireplace. He built a fire for her, he turned on the jets behind the little faux log in the faux marble gas fireplace, in his parents' avocado and gold living room in Larchmont. The seventies were almost over, but you wouldn't have known it at the Feinstadts'. He lit the fireplace in July with the air-conditioning turned up as high as it could be. He ripped the Marimekko duvet off his parents' bed and bore it back to her like a loud cheery silk-screened gift. They snuggled down beneath it, on the white rug – please don't let me leave a stain, thought Louise, please God, Jesus; she thought 'Jesus' while lying naked on the white rug of the local rabbi after an entire afternoon of teenage fornication with the local rabbi's only son – they even toasted marshmallows and drank hot chocolate . . . or now was she just embellishing? Who knew? This was the memory Louise conjured, years ago in her lonely dorm room, when she was still trapped like a solitary moth by the sticky-sweet nectar of her mourning, when she still got drunk on it; and then once in a while during the passing years whenever she and Peter had hit a rough patch and she dug around her dating memory for some better than average moments to compare him to. 'I always look back, too,' said Missy, over the phone with sympathy, the one time Louise had started to confess this to her, this penchant for comparing Peter to anything and everything, trying to keep him coming up short – 'Miss, when you're with Marcos, do you ever think of your old boyfriends?' 'Are you kidding?' said Missy. 'It's all Marcos and I ever talk about.'

'Marcos? You tell this stuff to Marcos?'

'Marcos spent the last few months hunting down some girl

he made out with in Bolivia when he was thirteen. Thirteen. Claudia Monte-something, Montenegro? Montezuma? When he was thirteen, Marcos made out with Claudia whatever, and he's never gotten over it. Never. He says he's thought about her every week for the last thirty-something years, and I know it's true, because for the past ten of them I've had to hear about her – *Cloud*ia Monte Hall. That's how he pronounces it, *Cloud*ia. Like she's goddamned celestial. Finally, I get sick of this shit and I say hunt her down hombre, and what does the fucker do, he hunts her down. Guess what, she's married to some software zillionaire up in Silicon Valley. So my husband? He calls her on the phone. Marcos. Mister Hard-to-Get, Mister-Never-Return-A-Phone-Call – even if it's from his kids, even if it's from his mother. He spends twenty minutes trying to make her remember who he is. He even brags about his movies . . . *Swampeater 2*, he brags about.'

'And?'

'And, I guess he wasn't that memorable. She had no idea who he was.'

'Poor Marcos.'

'Poor me. It's all I think about, old boyfriends. They're the reason I get up in the morning, the reason I comb my hair, the reason I still wear makeup. I'm always hoping I'll run into some old boyfriend, and he'll think, "Shit, she looks good. Why did I ever let her go?" '

'Don't you ever dream about meeting someone new?' asked Louise.

'God, no,' said Missy. 'I've been married too long. Men. I'm completely over them.'

Was Louise over men too?

Absolutely not.

Now, there was F. Scott, and he had left the AC in her apartment cranked as high as it could go in order to welcome her home from work. Was this a missive from the beyond, heaven sent, or just another spoiled boy's way of proving that he was cool? A dozen cheap roses from the Korean market stood, already wilting, in a glass jar on her coffee table. Underneath them was a torn page of loose-leaf lined with runny ink. There was a sketch of a cat on the paper.

'For you,' it said, 'from me.'

Under the picture he'd written BUSTER! and attached it to the sketch with a little scrawled-in arrow.

I should kill myself, thought Louise. She kicked off her shoes. Padded into the kitchen. Spritzed herself a glass of seltzer from one of the old-time seltzer bottles both she and Peter had delivered. They arrived in her apartment biweekly – Peter and she split the difference – brought by the Seltzer Man, an old guy, with a truss around his waist, the heavy wooden case resting on his shoulders, breaking his back. The company's name was Gimmee Seltzer, which was almost enough to make Louise cancel her order whenever she made out her monthly check, to the world's oldest, most hobbled delivery boy, to the enterprise with the worst cootchey-coo of a name, except that Louise was enamored of the bottles. Thick solid glass, as blue-green as the sea. It was one of the primary pleasures of living in New York, instead of some nice place like Seattle, those beach-glass bottles with their handsome silver handles.

She sat down cross-legged on her sofa. Began to list reasons for not killing herself, a favorite pastime she'd discovered after her divorce, during that awful period when she'd realized that getting rid of Peter hadn't solved exactly everything. *It didn't solve exactly anything. It was a stupid selfish move guaranteeing spinsterhood and childlessness and many equally terrible things.* What could be equally terrible? *Heartbreak. Heartbreak at your advanced age, lovebug.* Well, yes and no, thought Louise, at least before heartbreak there is possibility. Possibility. It was always number 1 on her list of reasons for continuing. What was it Sammy kept saying since he'd come home from rehab? Don't give up five minutes before the miracle.

Number 2: Food. All the foods of the world she never dared to eat that Peter was enamored of – drunken crabs, foie gras terrine, black truffles, sea urchins, numerous other items from the wet crawly floor of the ocean. Super-rich hot fudge sundaes – which she'd tasted, but never allowed herself to indulge in fully. Things she had never allowed herself to indulge in fully – they were a reason for being. The hope that someday, some way, she would.

Number 3: She'd never been to China. Plenty of slimy delicacies in China. In China there was a Great Wall. *Chinese babies. Orphanages full of them. Little girls who would be better off even with a single mother –* Mom again. Richard Nixon had gone to China. *I sure saw through that twisted little toad of a man. Who could forget what he did to Helen Gaghen Douglas?* In China they forgot the McCarthy era, but they didn't forget Richard Nixon. Missy had hooted over the sweatshirts sold in the marketplace 'next to the live chickens,' with pictures of his ugly mug ironed on them; she'd even given Louise one for her last birthday.

Missy and Marcos had been to China for a film festival. *Her husband took her.*

Reason to live number 4: It would kill her mother; it would kill Mom Silverstein if Louise Harrington killed herself. Even as tough as she was, *tough enough to stand up and speak out against Richard Nixon, not even Bobby Kennedy was that tough during the McCarthy era,* Mom couldn't live without her Louise.

Number 5: Sammy would get all the inheritance.

Number 6: There was always that book she could not write, the French she couldn't speak, that aria she'd never learn to sing. She sipped her seltzer. So far Louise was traversing a familiar list. A list she knew by heart. Fancy hotels with room service and Frette sheets. Anything could happen at any time. World peace. There could be world peace. A reversal in the Manhattan real estate market. The eradication of disease!

Number 7: Always a stickler, number 7. Louise always stopped herself short here and opened up a box of SnackWell's. Finally, now she had found a seventh reason. The mystery of F. Scott. Cracking it.

He had seen her painting. His painting. He had seen the painting that he himself had painted for her such a long, long time ago.

What did he really think when he saw that painting?

Number 7½. Finding out the answer to that question.

Number 8: The pleasures of a man who could still come twice within an hour. Who cared who he really was?

Number 9: With the reemergence of Scott Feinstadt or the emergence of F. Scott, either way, with the pleasures of a man who could still come twice, with a body that didn't slide, the fact that once again God was stuffing down her throat the idea that anything was possible.

Possibility; now she'd circled back to number 1. Food . . .

Her phone rang.

Louise leapt up, banging her shinbone against the coffee table.

'Fucking shit,' said Louise, as she hopped her way over to the phone.

She picked up just as the answering machine kicked in. Hmm, had he reconnected it? Erased all her messages? Had he spent the morning listening in? The machine let out such a high-pitched screech Louise thought she heard her neighbor's dog yowling along with it.

'Yeow,' said Missy, as Louise shouted hello into the receiver over the din.

Her finger found the stop button, and she hopped back with the phone into the living room.

'Take a pill, Missy, why don't you,' shouted Louise.

'You don't have to shout,' said Missy.

'Sorry,' said Louise.

'I was just going to give you a little treat and tell you about my pool boy. He doesn't wear a shirt and when he skims the scum off the water, he leans over and I can see the crack of his ass. Oooh-la-la!' said Missy.

'Say,' said Louise, remembering a variation on the same conversation – wasn't that the sum of her personal history with Missy, a thousand and one variations on the same conversation, boy talk? – 'Did you ever hear from Roger, the banker?'

'Did I hear from him, whooh boy,' said Missy. 'He sounded

middle-aged and lonely and horny. He said he was fat and his wife was always at the gym. His kids hate him. What a prize,' said Missy.

'Too bad,' said Louise.

'Yeah, too bad I didn't have the guts to go through with it,' said Missy.

What?

'We agreed to meet,' Missy said. 'I figured, I'm fat, he's fat, one person's fat would cancel out the other's. So we picked a time, a hotel. A hotel lobby. He was supposedly coming into town on business. What business? He's too rich to actually conduct business any more. He's hired a thousand and one people to do it for him – whatever. We agreed. A hotel lobby. Behind his back, Little Miss Slut here, I'd already booked the room,' Missy sighed.

A hotel. A hotel lobby and a room. Was Missy serious? Louise would never have done something like that when she was married. No matter how miserable she was. Single, she would have done it. Single, she would have done it with a middle-aged married fat man, but not when she herself was somebody else's wife. Well, that wasn't true, she'd actually done something like it (cheated) a few times herself – sad, pathetic gropings with a colleague in a closet at an end-of-semester party, that stranger she'd met on a plane (Italian, bad teeth) and his airport hotel room, after a particularly harrowing weekend with her father and her two delinquent step-brothers down in Florida when Peter was in LA at a conference, that jazz musician who had given her the clap. There had been a time when things were so wrong between her and Peter, so strangely, undefinably, specifically wrong between them – to this day it was hard to put her finger on it, why two attractive, intelligent people who got along as well as they seemed to, could live a life so lonely – that she'd resorted to these brief trespasses just to prove to herself that she was still a sexual being.

'So it was your feelings for Marcos that stopped you?' said Louise, somewhat bitterly, full of envy.

'Marcos? Hell no. Marcos said to go for it,' said Missy.

'Marcos told you to go for it?' Now it was Louise who positively screeched.

'Yeah, can you believe it?' said Missy. 'That asshole. He said, "Maybe if you scratch your eetch, you won't be such a beetch." The bastard. He's got some kind of foreign rhyming disease. No, Marcos practically pimped me. It was yours truly who pulled the plug.'

'Why, Miss?' asked Louise.

'The last time I slept with Roger, I was twenty-two, and, well, I hadn't exactly had two kids – know what I'm saying? I mean, you should see my tits. They hang down to my knees. I could be on the cover of *National Geographic*. How could I ever explain my water bra?'

'Your what?'

'It's like a waterbed; it holds them high and jiggly.'

Louise looked down at the phone.

'You're kidding, right? And I thought you said Roger was fat, anyway.'

'He was always fat,' said Missy. 'Back then, I had knockers.'

Louise sighed. Louise had never had knockers. 'Oh, come on Miss, you always needed a bra.'

'You're getting laid, aren't you,' said Missy, the blood-hound. Could she be Mom's illegitimate offspring?

'What?' said Louise.

'You always get mean to me when you're getting laid,' said Missy.

Was it true?

'Who is he?'

'I don't know,' said Louise, confessing.

Missy sucked in her breath. She puffed it out.

'Is he old and rich?' asked Missy, breathlessly.

'No,' said Louise.

'Fuck,' said Missy. 'He's young and poor. You lucky girl. I hate your fucking guts, Louise.'

If you only knew, thought Louise.

'You're not answering,' said Missy. 'You're fucking a penniless actor, no, a writer, God no, you're fucking a god-damned starving artist.'

There was silence on the line.

'I hate my life,' said Missy.

Was it true? Did Missy really hate the life that Louise so coveted?

'As God is my witness,' said Missy, sounding like Scarlett O'Hara, 'I wish that I were you.'

———◆———

That night, Louise and Peter met up on her corner, in front of the Korean grocer's. Peter's favorite bum was outside, an elderly Hispanic man who carried a sign that said that he was brain-damaged from falling on his head – if he were so brain-damaged, how had he written that sign? As Louise rounded the corner, she saw the two of them, silhouetted in the streetlights, Peter's hand in his pocket, digging out some change.

'Here,' she heard Peter say, 'that's all I have today.'

The bum rained on Peter some sweet, organic gibberish.

'Get yourself something to eat,' said Peter, her Peter. 'A slice of pizza, how about it?'

'Sounds good,' said Louise, sidling up behind him, slipping her arm through his.

'What?' said Peter, looking at her with surprise, the beginnings of a smile lighting up his handsome face.

'I was just thinking some nice slice pizza would hit the spot.'

It had been a long time since she'd been nice to Peter. Louise gave his arm a little squeeze. The gesture caught them both by surprise, and the pleasure it caused shuddered through them like a mutually satisfying sexual maneuver. That rare.

'Hmmm,' he said. 'What ever I'm doing right, let's both hope I keep on doing it.'

Indeed, thought Louise.

'You do a lot of things right,' said Louise, emphatically. 'You're a good man, Peter.' She felt wholly grateful for his goodness in the moment that she said this.

'Aaah, the old good man routine,' said Peter, but he was smiling for real now. He tucked her arm against his side a little tighter. 'The old kiss-of-death phrase.'

Isn't it amazing, Louise thought, how good Peter always

ends up looking when juxtaposed against just about any other man? It was his confidence and authority that most appealed to her.

She pressed her cheek against his shoulder.

The night was cool and luminous. Broadway glowed in the smoggy, springy haze. They walked arm in arm down the avenue, a gentle wind whipping up the trash.

'Beer or Cokes?' Peter whispered into her hair. The moisture from his breath warmed her part.

'Cokes,' said Louise, feeling safe.

They bypassed the Korean market. They headed into Sal & Carmine's. The last good slice pizza joint in the city. No whole-wheat crust, no charcoal-fired ovens. Just salty cheese and old-fashioned spaghetti sauce.

'Good evening,' said Peter. 'Two slices, plain. Two Cokes. One classic for me and a diet for the lady.'

He was masterful at this, at ordering. Louise looked on him with love. She marveled at the way he dug into his suit pants.

'Let's box it, okay?' said Louise. 'Take it back to my place?' She squeaked the question out into his shoulder.

'Okay,' said Peter. His voice strong and deep. 'That sounds great.'

In the gray-blue urban light that passed itself off as a sunset, Peter looked solid, steady, mature. No tattoos for Peter, paid for by his parents' hard-earned money. No Calvin Klein waistband peeking above his belt, no gangbanger shorts. He was actually wearing a lightweight jacket. Seersucker. Something she'd helped him pick out at Brooks Brothers. He looked like a real, live man.

The pizza was cold by the time Peter and Louise had strolled back to Louise's apartment, but Louise didn't care. She put it out congealed and glistening with oil on two of her best china wedding plates. She went into the linen closet and sprung out two folded linen napkins. She went back into the kitchen and unearthed a bottle of red wine – a spicy Cabernet. She opened her glass cabinet in order to search out two wine goblets, but what she saw took her breath away. A bakery box. A bakery box empty save for a perfect chocolate cupcake – capped by a cone of lucious mocha frosting. Next to it a little note – 'To make your dreams sweet' – and a little Hershey's kiss.

F. Scott.

When it rains, it pours.

Wasn't it funny, how when things were happening with one guy it made things possible with another? It was like being offered a job while you are already gainfully employed. The men rain from the sky like manna.

Dizzy, she made her way back to Peter.

Isn't this great, she thought, I'm cheating on F. Scott. I'm cheating on my husband.

How can you cheat if you're not in a relationship with either one of them?

I'm not listening, thought Louise. My internal hands are over my internal ears.

Louise sat down cross-legged before her coffee table and faced her husband. Her ex. Even F. Scott had found the prefix sexy. She forwent the cokes and poured them both a glass of wine. 'So,' she said, 'Peter, tell me about your day.'

Tell me about yours and I'll tell you about mine.

The tops of Peter's ears turned pink. She couldn't remember them ever doing that before. In fact, his cheeks also took on a mild flush.

'Peter,' said Louise. 'What are you blushing about?' But she said it with confidence, knowing in the moment that he felt as attracted to her as she felt to him, that after all that time, together and apart, they were once again, miraculously, finding that special spark between them.

But instead of taking her into his arms as she expected, Peter choked on his wine, turned an incandescent purple.

'Peter? Do you need the Heimlich?'

'No, no, Lou,' he sputtered. 'I'm fine.' He pounded his fist against his chest. Which seemed to steady him, the art of self-flagellation.

'In fact,' he said, 'I'm good.'

'Good,' said Louise.

'Good,' said Peter.

Earth to my Louise.

'Good?' said Louise.

'Yes,' said Peter.

Her heart, it did not flutter, instead it began to sink. Had she misinterpreted him? Wasn't she old enough now, wise enough now, to realize that just because she felt one way, just because she felt strongly, it didn't automatically mean her partner did as well?

'I mean, I guess you can guess it, I'm sure you already know. I'm seeing somebody. I mean, I'm actually seeing one person.'

Well, you wouldn't be seeing one dog, would you now, thought Louise. But she said nothing. So the tables had turned on her. Again. Stupid girl, to open up and be vulnerable.

'And I guess you can guess it, I mean I guess you can guess who it is. I'm sure it's written all over my face.'

'The only thing all over your face is cold tomato sauce,' said Louise. It just slipped out of her.

Peter wiped his chin with one of her linen napkins. A napkin she would now have to wash and iron. Shit. She'd wasted a linen napkin on Peter.

'Farrah?' squeaked out Louise.

Peter nodded, trying not to look too pleased.

'A student?' asked Louise, struggling to keep the edge out of her voice.

'Well, it worked for me before,' said Peter, a little too jocularly for Louise's liking. He didn't have to get cocky about it. 'Besides, she's not my student. She's getting a joint degree in international business and maritime law. She's just my employee,' said Peter.

It's still sexual harassment, Louise wanted to scream, but instead, she said: 'I'm glad for you.'

'Thank you, Louise, that's large of you.'

Large? she thought. Large? Little do you know but I spent all last night spilling love juice with an angel on the exact same spot of the carpet where you've just parked your doughy ass!

She didn't say any of this.

She was gracious.

Good girl!

They sat together quietly for a moment.

Then Peter gave a little cough.

'Yes?' said Louise.

Peter looked at her.

There's more.

'There's more?'

'There's more, Lou,' said Peter.

Louise got up, went into the kitchen and reached for her emergency pack. Nestled on top of the box of Marlboros was a little marijuana joint wrapped with a tiny ribbon. Another present from F. Scott.

'I had lunch with Sammy today.'

Louise reached for the doobie and the nicotine.

'He's got this in, this DVD company – you know, DVDs on the back of the headrests of SUVs, so the kiddies can sit out long car trips, DVDs you can rent in airport lounges, DVDs set up in shopping carts – anywhere kids go and need to be occupied. We deliver some of the seed money, and then we get a guaranteed IPO.' Peter was serious. 'The real trick is that I'd have to cash in my 401K and just about everything else we own to qualify as an initial investor. I mean actually, we'd have to borrow . . .'

'Borrow?' said Louise. 'Borrow? From whom exactly would we borrow?'

'From Sammy, of course,' said Peter.

Was he nuts?

'Are you nuts, Peter? Have you lost your mind? This doesn't sound anything like you.' And it didn't. It really didn't. The Peter she knew wouldn't never be willing to risk everything he'd worked for on a gambler's roll of the dice. 'Sammy's totally unreliable, you know that,' said Louise. 'For god's sake, he's an addict, who knows what he'd do with that mon—'

'He's in recovery,' said Peter. He said it the way he might have said, 'Case-closed.'

'So what,' said Louise.

'So he's a different person now,' said Peter. He was calm when he said this, but his ears were now the pinkest she'd ever seen. Red. They were redder than her lipstick. 'I've studied the proposal carefully and the deal is sound.' Peter was convinced. Now, he would convince her, too. 'These days, Sammy's a different man.'

'What do you know from Sammy?' said Louise.

'We've been spending some time together. We've been talking.'

Peter and Sammy?

'I've been talking with Sammy,' said Peter. 'God,' he said, 'it felt good to let that out.'

Louise was confused.

'Let out what?' said Louise.

Peter looked at her. His eyes were hard. Why were they so hard? His focus narrowed. 'I'll tell you if you want to know,' he said. 'If you're ready.' He said it like a challenge.

Ready? Ready for what? All of a sudden Louise wanted to smoke. A cigarette, a banana leaf, anything.

'Hey, Pete,' said Louise. 'Want to blow a joint? If you blow a joint with me, I'll be ready to hear all about you and Sammy going behind my back.'

'We didn't go behind your back, Louise. We went in front of your face.'

Peter didn't exactly sound belligerent here, but he did sound confrontational. Somehow, the current openess between them had given him a way to find fresh courage.

Peter had never sounded confrontational before. What was going on?

At the very least, Louise could see, she could see that much, it was going to be a long, strange evening. She didn't want to face it sober. She didn't want Peter, this new, hard-as-nails Peter, to notice the peculiar shaking in her knees.

She waved the joint temptingly in the air.

'That's a good idea,' said Peter, surprising her. Peter never, ever got wasted. 'Because there's more, Lou. God. God. This really is beginning to feel right, finally. Finally. I'm finally ready to tell you everything.'

Louise fired up F. Scott's joint. She took a big hit, then passed it onto her ex-husband. He took a drag and held the smoke for a long time in his lungs, long enough for Louise to realize that nobody ever knew anybody really – when did Peter learn how to smoke a joint? She'd always flaunted this little pleasure of hers; by lighting up defiantly in front of him when they were first together, him tenderly worrying over the chemical effects of cannabis on the tissue of her pink young lungs – that was back when he still really cared about her. Or by hiding it from him when they were older, when he didn't care so much any longer, just saw her little dalliances as some further sign of Louise's contempt. By then Louise would smoke her pot alone in the park by the river, but return home in time to let Peter detect the smell of the sweet dense smoke on her hair and sweater, to slap him in the face with it. The trouble was, after a while, Peter didn't notice. All this time, Louise thought she was the only one in the room, in the small dark claustrophobic little room of their marriage, who liked to indulge in this specific tiny pleasure. Nobody knew anybody else, really. Why, one could spend fourteen years of her life with a veritable stranger. And that stranger sitting across the room from her, that straight, smart, overly controlled Peter Harrington, was holding the pot smoke down deep in his lungs like an old stoner pro hanging out at her high school football stadium. Nobody knew anybody, Louise included. She didn't know the first thing about either one of them.

<hr />

It began before he met her. It began before he met her even. In high school. In college. By the time he'd arrived in Ithaca, he was hopeless.

Hopeless?

Hopelessly addicted.

To what? To what, Pete?

Reefers. Heroin. Drugs? What else are people addicted to?

Grief.

Grief?

I'm addicted to grief, Mom.

You're addicted to stasis. You're addicted to the past. You can't let go of anything, Louise. You never could.

For Peter, it was none of the above.

'Sex,' said Peter, softly, so softly, the word came out like a little exhalation of breath. Like a cloud. That damn sex cloud. It floated out of Peter's mouth, hovered in the air. It sat pregnant and damp, hanging over Louise.

'Sex?' said Louise.

'Sex,' said Peter.

'I hadn't noticed,' Louise said.

Sex. Her Peter. He was addicted to sex. That is, he was addicted to sex, it seemed, with anyone else but his wife. His wife, Louise.

'I couldn't stop having sex. Sex with women, mostly. Girls,' said Peter. 'I like girls. You know, girls of age,' he quickly added. 'Females, I should say. I prefer women,' said Peter. He took a breath. 'Although,' he added, 'I have tried other things.'

'Other things?' Louise repeated this.

'You know,' said Peter. But she didn't. Other things meant what, men, children, dogs?

'Men,' said Peter. 'A few of them.'

What the hell did that mean?

'What the hell does that mean?' asked Louise.

It was dark in her apartment, the room was frozen, Louise was frozen, Peter hadn't moved it seemed in minutes, but still the world was spinning. It was as if Peter and Louise were the axis and everyone else moved in space around them. Sure, there was no progress for the rest – the entire earthly population – they were spinning in circles, after all; they were born, grew, dreamed, fell in love, were disappointed, found some pleasure, got older, died; but at least they were actually moving. Peter and Louise were stationary, trapped by their own specific marital sludge, like insects in cooling amber. Peter sat on the floor, his legs slightly splayed out before him beneath her coffee table, his back up against the couch. He was looking down at his own knees. This isn't happening, thought Louise. But of course it was. Everything significant that ever happened in her life felt like it wasn't happening in the very moment when it most undoubtedly and irrevocably was.

She remembered now the phone call, the summer following her junior year in high school. She'd been lying in her little single bed staring out the window. The leaves on the old flaming maple outside were the deepest end-of-summer green. They were so purely, totally green, she'd just noted, that no wonder they'd have to brown and crumple and fall off. No one, no thing, could be so purely and totally at the pinnacle of their being, no one, no thing, could exist so fully as themselves for very long without completely giving out. This is what Louise was thinking back then, when the phone rang.

It was Missy.

She was breathing heavily. 'Wheezy,' she said, 'I'm having an anxiety attack.' She said, 'Tell me, are we still best friends, are we still best friends for life, you and me? I mean, you're still mine. Tell me I'm yours, Wheezy, please.'

Louise hadn't even bothered to roll over or sit up; she just lay on her stomach staring at the world's greenest tree. The truth was she hadn't had the strength for movement. In her head she said: You have to be kidding. Missy. Best friends? You and me? You took the one boy I'll ever love, you took him away from me. Enemies. Enemies is more like it. But she didn't say any of this. Instead, she twirled the corkscrew curls of her phone cord around and around her finger.

'Please,' breathed Missy.

'What's wrong?' asked Louise.

'It's Scott,' said Missy, 'Oh God.' She could barely speak.

Are you kidding? thought Louise. Now you're going to complain to me? What, he's cheated on you, he's left you, he forgot to send you flowers on your birthday? Am I supposed to instantly slip back into my best friend role, because the guy you stole from me, just did you dark? Don't you realize all I do is think about him? I haven't moved from obsession to reminiscence yet. I'm too young now to even know that that kind of emotional shift is possible – did Louise think this in the moment, or again, was this just experience talking? I'm too young now to know that if pain were helium and the skin of my soul were a balloon, with the nature of this pain, it would fill the entire space, and only over the years would some of it leak out. I'm too young now to know that over time I will forget how I feel, that I will be able to see Scott Feinstadt for the very cute jerk he was. No, that was hindsight talking. Hindsight and bad metaphors. Then, all Louise could think to say, to say to herself, to say to Missy inside her head, was: I'm still in pain here. Thinking about Scott Feinstadt is for me like being green is for these stupid leaves. I do it purely and totally. I live and breathe him. I'm still in pain here, Missy.

'What about him?' said Louise.

'He's dead,' said Missy. 'Oh, God, Louise.'

At the time, Louise had thought, none of this is really happening. She'd continued twirling the corkscrew curls of the phone cord around her middle finger.

Now, two decades later, at home in her apartment with Peter, Louise thought, none of this is happening, even while she asked her husband the names of the men he'd been with, the men whose dicks had been in his mouth, the men who had put those same dicks up his ass, worse, the men he'd slept with and woken up with the next morning, the men who perhaps even shared the very same pillow with him. The men her husband had kissed.

'Dave Shearson, Dave Weinstock, Dave Kovacs.'

'Only men named Dave?' said Louise. She was trying to be funny, but it came out angry. Or was she trying to be angry and it came out funny? Whatever she was trying to be, it came out something different.

'Derrick,' said Peter.

Derrick. Peter's engineer geek roommate back in Ithaca. Derrick. Peter's roommate when she'd met him.

'Oh, so your fetish is the letter D?'

'Well, no,' said Peter, quietly. 'It isn't.'

No such luck.

'But that's the least of it,' said Peter. 'There weren't that many, men, I mean. And I stopped that, a long time ago.'

'The least of it?' repeated Louise.

'Echolalia,' said Peter.

'Echolalia?' said Louise.

'You're repeating everything I say,' said Peter. He said it softly. With regret. 'I guess this hurts you, hunh?'

'You might say that,' said Louise. 'I guess this hurts me, hunh.'

She got up, went over to the counter, and lit a cigarette.

Peter sighed, shifted his position. Went cross-legged, sort of, cross-legged for Peter. Limber wasn't exactly his middle name. This sexual athlete. He could barely tie his own shoes.

When they were married, when she'd still liked him, she used to clip his toenails for him. Even after their divorce, she'd do it for him when he asked.

'Who, how many, when, that's not the point, Lou.'

Who? Guys whose names started with the letter *D*. How many? Not that many, said Peter. Not that many, when just anecdotally, from this meager conversation, it seemed that Peter had slept with more men in his spare time than Louise had, devoting much of her life to this very same pursuit. When? She hadn't even had the time yet to wrap her head around what he'd just confessed, hadn't had the time yet to ask herself this extremely obvious and salient question. Well, now that he'd brought it up . . .

'Let me get this straight. You did these things with other people while you were still with me?' Louise blew these last ten words out in staccato blasts like a series of rapidfire smoke rings.

'Yes,' said Peter. 'I did.'

'You did these things with other people even after you'd stopped doing them with me?'

'Yes,' said Peter.

Let's turn back the page, thought Louise. Let's go back another chapter. I don't want to know from this, I don't want to know from anything. I'm not even your wife any more. I'm not even your wife any more! Why do I have to know such things?

'I'm not even your wife any more . . .' she started, but then she ran out of steam.

Peter looked her dully in the eye. His gaze hit her iris like a spray of spit. It made her blink.

'That's why. That's why you're not my wife any more. You're not my wife any more because I was addicted to having sex with other people.'

Oh. She'd thought she was not his wife any more because she'd grown bored of him. She'd thought she was not his wife any more because she only had one life to live and life with Peter hadn't exactly felt like living. She'd thought she wasn't his wife any more because she'd left *him*.

'I was so guilt ridden all the time, I completely shut down. Farrah's taught me that.'

Farrah?

'We met at a twelve-step program. Sammy introduced us, and when we had an opening in the department, I hired her.'

'Sammy?' said Louise.

'Yeah. Eventually, I turned to Sammy. I figured if anyone ever knew anything about addiction, it was him. And he was family.'

Whose family? thought Louise. He was her brother, but she'd never, ever thought of Sammy as family. Her mother was her family. And Peter. Peter and Mom, family, period. Dad was that tall, stoop-shouldered man who sometimes seemed to roam around their living room and now lived with a pretty nurse and her two greaser sons in Florida for God's sake. In Florida, where old people go. Old people and clothing designers and models. Her father lived with this motley crew by choice. By choice over Mom and Louise. Dad was a Fellini movie. Family, hunh. So Sammy was in on this with Peter.

'I needed help, Lou. Sammy helped me. He listened to me.

116

He took me to twelve steps. And Farrah, she gave me the courage to make it work.'

They were all like a little club, Sammy, Farrah, Peter. All against Louise. Leaving her out of the loop.

'I guess I should thank him,' Louise said, a little bitterly. 'I guess this is the part where I'm supposed to call up Sammy and thank him for taking my husband away from me.'

'He didn't take me away, Lou. He's helping me to find my way back. He's helped me so much. Even this financial thing – why it's the tip of the iceberg of the ways Sammy has helped me.' Peter paused. 'You know, we really could make a lot of money.'

Just Louise's luck; now Peter the recovered ex would turn into Peter the millionaire.

Oh, who cared?

'I don't think about money,' said Louise.

'I know. That's why Sammy and I are doing the thinking for you. I want to protect you, Louise. It's the least I can do. It's the least I can do after everything . . .' Peter looked so ashamed, he looked so ashamed of himself in the moment. '. . . after everything else I've done –'

'Oh my God,' Louise interrupted him. She began to cry. For the first time it seemed in years. Tear water was running down her cheeks.

'Oh my God, you're on step nine, aren't you? You're on goddamn fucking step nine. God,' said Louise, blowing her nose into the handkerchief Peter produced for her. The same fucking handkerchief she'd bought him for their former anniversary. 'I thought I'd never have to live through that again.'

Fucking step nine, when the addict makes reparations. Sammy's last step nine had almost killed their mother. Sammy's step nine – when the least of his confessions was about how he had frequented crack houses and stolen money from all of them.

Louise hated step nine with a passion.

'What did I do, to make you behave this way?' said Louise.

Peter's head snapped back. It was as if she had slapped him in the face.

'You? None of it ever had anything to do with you, Lou.'

How could that be? How could the fact that Peter wanted to have sex with everyone else on the planet but her, not have anything to do with Louise?

'I loved you. I love you still.'

'You love me?' asked Louise. It was the first question out of her mouth that whole horrible evening that really felt like a question, and not like another statement, a statement with a little fillip of sound at the end, an upswing, a statement that had sprouted wings.

'Yes,' said Peter. 'I did. And I do. That's why I have to come clean. Farrah said. She said if there was ever going to be any hope for her and me, I had to come clean with Louise, with my wife. And so that's what I'm doing. I'm coming clean, Louise. In my own peculiar way, I'm still in love with you.'

———◆———

Peter left that night when it was morning. Three o'clock in the morning to be precise. He left because Louise threw him out.

She threw him out, because after his rather long, involved, detailed confession, he'd fallen asleep on the floor beside her couch. She had been speechless, speechless for quite some time, so the apartment was quiet. Dark and quiet. And he was spent. After about twenty minutes of watching him sleep – how could he sleep at a time like that? – Louise had kicked him a little in the ribs.

'Peter?' said Louise, kicking.

'Hmmph?' said Peter.

'Get the hell out of my house, you bastard.'

At three o'clock in the morning, Louise Harrington kicked Professor Peter Harrington in the ribs and threw him out of her house. He went quietly and reluctantly, but Louise had the sneaking suspicion that once he got out to the sidewalk he did a little dance. Of victory? Of freedom? Who knows; it only existed in her imagination, this dance, Peter, arms raised, hips wiggling, doing a little soca humpty-hump. Most of Louise's life, it now seemed, had existed only in her imagination. Was that true for everybody else on the planet, that their lives were something they constructed inside their heads?

No.

No?

No, Louise. You're the only one.

Once Peter was gone, Louise's apartment was even darker and more quiet than it had been before. Wasn't that the sum of it, her whole stupid history with Peter? When he was gone, her apartment was even more dark and quiet than it was when he was home.

Louise picked up the phone. It was now 3:15 in the

---

morning. She called the only person she could think to call at that hour. It was only midnight in Southern California.

Missy picked up on the third ring.

'Louise?'

Louise couldn't speak.

'Louise, I know it's you. I've got caller ID. Louise?'

Louise tried to answer her but she couldn't find the words.

'Oh Wheezy, what did that boy do to you?'

How did she know? thought Louise. How come everyone knows everything but me? *You don't want to know, honey.* She thought this while she was hyperventilating. She thought this because she still could not summon up enough oxygen to speak.

'Those fucking starving artists. He picked up the phone the other day when I was trying to reach you.'

She was talking about F. Scott. Not Peter. Missy had talked to him. Alarms went off, ringing inside Louise's head. Had Missy recognized his voice?

'He sounded like a nice enough kid, but I saw right through him.'

Missy saw right through him? What did she see when she saw right through F. Scott? Blood and bones, a proper skeleton? Or was there nothing there, because they'd managed to conjure him up out of their collective imagination?

Missy said: 'I love you, sweetchick, you know?'

For the second time in a very long time, for the second time that very morning, Louise began to weep. To really weep. It was raining on her face. In the background, Missy murmured one silly endearment after another. A mother, she was practiced now in the art of comforting. A mother, she was practiced now in comforting her charge for the wrong thing. No starving artist had broken Louise's heart, no blast from the past, no fantasy boy re-created like a golem. This time the job had been done correctly, by her own husband.

'Oh God, Miss. It's Peter. The bastard. He cheated on me.'

She could almost feel Missy's glee.

'No one could love you more than me,' murmured Missy.

Any more love tonight and Louise would need a head-stone.

——◆——

It was five o'clock the next evening when F. Scott Feinstadt showed up at her door. Louise was still in her pajamas. That is, Louise was still in the silky shirt F. Scott had laid out for her yesterday morning. She hadn't gone to sleep. She hadn't gone to work. She hadn't showered even. She hadn't done anything but smoked cigarettes. And ignored her mother's messages – that motherfucker Peter hadn't called. *Darling, it's been so long since I've talked to you.* Twenty-four hours, Mom. A world record. And listened to music. Joni Mitchell. Even that didn't help. Why hadn't he called her? He always called her. He'd called her every day since the first time they'd slept together, even just to nag. Joni Mitchell sang: 'I wish I had a river, I could skate away on . . .' It had helped when Scott Feinstadt died, but not now.

'Baby,' said F. Scott, when she opened the door after a series of prolonged rings.

He said 'Baby' to a woman who hadn't even brushed her teeth. 'What's wrong, sweet Louise?'

Before she knew it she was sobbing wetly in his arms, with the door to her apartment open, for all her neighbors to see.

F. Scott led her gently over to the sofa, kicking the door shut behind them.

'Shshsh, baby, baby, baby,' he said into her hair, as he held her, letting the sobs rock through her, out of her body and into his chest. 'Shshsh, baby, baby, baby,' as he physically absorbed all her disappointment and anger and grief. He was a sponge, this boy. He took her world upon his shoulders, he soaked her pain up into his kidneys. When she was done, finally, she pulled her head away from his chest and noticed a little puddle of drool, her drool, on F. Scott's T-shirt, like a bulls-eye, right above his heart. She tried to wipe it away quickly with her hand, but only succeeded in spreading the stuff.

'Now tell me,' said F. Scott. 'Does this have anything to do with me?'

The narcissist.

'Oh, God no. It's Peter, my husband, he came over last night, and well, he finally told me some stuff, you know, some stuff I wouldn't want to know, I mean it's all ancient history, the stuff, him and me, I mean, I don't know why I give a shit . . .'

F. Scott nodded. 'Like when you were married, maybe he did a little cheating?'

Louise nodded. Her lower lip began to tremble. But how did he know?

'So this *is* all about me,' said F. Scott.

'Hunh?' said Louise.

'He could smell me,' said F. Scott. 'He could smell how I've entered your bloodstream. He's jealous. He wants you back.'

'You think?' said Louise. This theory put a nice new twist on things. Why not see Peter's confession as a form of flattery? It worked better than seeing it as the fucking hostile attack it really was.

'Just drop kick the guy, okay? Just tell him to get lost.'

Louise sat up. F. Scott was so oddly possessive about her, when for all practical purposes, they'd just met.

'But you and I, we've just met . . .' said Louise, then her voice started to trail off. Had they just met, or had they known each other all along?

'I know,' said F. Scott. 'That's the weird part. We've just met.' He stopped here to contemplate the weight of his last sentence. 'But, Louise, I swear to God, I feel like I've known you for ever. Whatever is going on,' and here F. Scott took her hand, 'whatever is going on between us, it's like it's got some magical component, some this-is-it-ness that I want to explore . . . and I don't want your ex getting proprietary and messing it up, just as we're getting started.'

She took her hand out of his and ran her fingers through her hair.

'Look, guys are dogs,' said F. Scott. 'We're animals.' F. Scott said to Louise. 'But with you I don't feel like a dog. I feel like a man.'

Louise stared at him. What was going on here? Was he really so taken with her? Was he playing some stupid courtship game? Or was he just a fucking nut?

It was as if F. Scott read her mind.

'I don't want to scare you. You want to go slow, I'll try and go slow.'

Louise looked up at him and nodded.

'So why don't you slowly go into the shower, because we have a date tonight, right? There is no past here, there's just you and me. And we can take our time. Am I right?'

When you're right you're right, thought Louise. No past. What a perfect, perfect thing. She got up. Headed for the bathroom. 'I'll only be a minute,' she said.

'Take as long as you want,' said F. Scott. 'Tonight is only about you and me.'

That's right. You and me. And a cast of thousands, thought Louise. More than the extras in *Ben-Hur*. Plus all their baggage. You idiot boy, you. You narcissist. You think you're my only living ghost.

———◆———

They had dinner together in a hole-in-the-wall restaurant in Chinatown. Wing Fat. F. Scott ordered the drunken crab, then left Louise alone with the fried wontons while he ran out and picked up a six of beers. In the ten minutes that he was gone, she ate all five wontons with her fingers, letting the oil run down her wrist to her arm before blotting the whole mess with her napkin. When he came back and saw the empty plate, F. Scott laughed and ordered another round. Then he gently took the napkin out of her hand and delicately licked her glistening fingers one by one, sitting down right next to Louise, not across from her, as if they were seated at a banquette in some formal fancy restaurant. Instead, they were sort of hunched over a slab of Formica, F. Scott working on her hands, Louise staring at their reflections in a gold-veined mirror. How cute they looked, thought Louise, as F. Scott licked away at her forefinger and her thumb. He was young and handsome and did a pretty good imitation of a guy who might be in love, or at least a guy who was hoping he might get some. Which was fine with Louise, the latter, it was fine with her to feel wanted. So she smiled at her own reflection, the gold veins disrupting her face rather flatteringly, giving her dimples even, and with the lines jogging her features just so, and if she squinted, that is if she almost totally closed her eyes and let them water, she looked like a pretty girl, a pretty young girl in her braid and peasant blouse and jeans and clogs – an outfit she'd seen on at least a dozen teenage girls this very same evening out on the street. Except that Louise's old jean jacket was just that, old, and theirs were stiff and indigo, as if the weave itself had been impregnated with a lot of dried, dark ink. Otherwise her young clothes were the same as their young clothes, except that theirs had probably cost a zillion dollars or had been unearthed from their mothers' closets, and Louise had just pilfered her own.

Nevertheless, in that gold-veined mirror and even under that harsh yellow lighting, she didn't look like somebody's mother. She looked like the handsome older woman F. Scott wanted to fuck. She smiled at herself. Dimples.

When the first round of dishes was finished, F. Scott perused the menu on the table under the yellowed stained Plexiglas and declared that he was still hungry – a growing boy. So he ordered spare ribs and soup dumplings and chow fun for himself, Louise declining, Louise declaring she could not stomach another bite. But when the dishes arrived, one overlapping the other like a musical scale up the waiter's arm, Louise ate all, sipping the liquid out of the dumplings the way F. Scott showed her, spiking each one with a burning dash of Chinese vinegar that traveled up her sinuses and singed her eyebrows from the inside. Plus, she drank three beers in record time. The alcohol and the MSG flushed her face, so that her own cheeks felt hot to her own palms, which were always icy. F. Scott grabbed one hand and kissed the palm as he talked, on and on, F. Scott talked and talked to Louise the whole time they were eating. When she tuned in, it was about art, again. About why he liked it. Art. F. Scott was talking about why he liked art, 'ART in capitals,' he said, 'art as a concept.' Certain paintings he saw in certain museums in certain European cities were capable of rearranging the molecules inside his blood – what the hell did that mean? He said he could physically feel the paintings entering him through his skin. 'Like you, Louise Harrington, I can feel you entering me – God, sometimes I wish I had a vagina.' The male member of an elderly couple from Long Island sitting across from them snorted at this, but his wife made hush-hush noises. Everyone likes to see young people in love, Louise thought. Even me. She gazed at the two of them again in her mirror, Louise and her art student. We look pretty damn cute, she thought. A little mismatched, but not weird. Not freakish, just kind of downtown and interesting, Louise decided. At one point, when F. Scott got past his 'gynophilia' spiel, as he called it, she ventured to speak. Rauschenberg, sure. But Robert Ryman. All that white. Agnes Martin. Why, Louise would be happy the rest of her life, she whispered, if she could wake up every morning to an Agnes Martin – those beautiful grids, like handwritten fields of color – drink coffee all day, and stare at it.

'You're amazing,' F. Scott said to her. 'That's exactly the way I feel about Agnes Martin, too. Her work is so pure, so beautiful.'

After dinner, F. Scott had to practically push Louise up the restaurant's steep steps on to the sidewalk – she was either that winded or that wasted, who knew? who cared? with his hands massaging her lower back like that – and then he took her out for Hong Kong bubble sodas, which she'd never had before, with tapioca pearls at the bottom that they both sucked up through their straws.

'I want to know everything about you,' said F. Scott, gravely, as they sat side by side, slurping at the counter. With his foot, he gave the stool next to his a little spin for emphasis.

Why? thought Louise, when there were so many, many things that she herself now wanted to forget.

'Like your favorite food; let me guess, sushi? Is it sushi, Louise? Sushi and black-and-white cookies? Not the shrink-wrapped ones you find in a deli, but the old-fashioned bakery kind?'

It was, it was.

'Color? Ecru, coffee, tan?'

How did he know?

'Band?' F. Scott said.

Band? thought Louise. Band?

She waited patiently to hear from F. Scott what indeed her favorite band was. Perhaps on this subject F. Scott could enlighten her – give her a little more insight into herself. She'd spent her whole life listening to whatever music whatever boyfriend had put on the stereo. But after a few moments it was clear, F. Scott didn't know either. The great mind reader was finally stumped.

He leaned in closer. His breath smelled like hops. He had the very same sweet, slightly fermented breath that cows do after an afternoon of grazing. How did Louise know from cows? Must have been that poet up in Ithaca, the one who took her to see the sheep; he must have shown her the whole goddamn farm – or was it Peter, Peter who had insisted on pulling his old Chevy over to the side of the road on the way home from a picnic and made her feed a brown-eyed Holstein some hay through an old wire fence? It must have been Peter who told her to close her eyes and breathe in that cow's wet, green, hoppy breath until she felt drunk, but who knew, one memory was bleeding into another. Soon it would all add up to the same stupid boy.

F. Scott breathed beer onto her face.

'Do you have a best friend?' F. Scott asked her, and when she opened her eyes, his were so probing, so insistent, she had to answer him.

'Why, yes, I do,' said Louise. 'Do you?'

'I did,' said F. Scott. 'This guy Ricky. We've been tight since orientation at art school. But he's a dickhead.'

Oh, thought Louise. 'Well, Missy's a dickhead too,' she said. 'But she's still my best friend.'

F. Scott looked at her with that same darkly curious look upon his face. 'Missy?'

What was the question? Louise decided to answer it anthropologically.

'It's a nickname a lot of Melissas had in the seventies.'

Oh. F. Scott's pupils dilated.

'Confession,' he said.

Hunh?

'I talked to her on the phone,' F. Scott said.

That's right. F. Scott talked to Missy. Why hadn't Louise paid attention to this salient fact before.

He looked down at the floor. 'The other day, when you were at work, she called,' he said. 'And then, ah, later, well, I called her back.'

He called her back?

'You don't mind, do you?'

It depended on what Missy had said to him. What *had* gone down between them? When the phone rang, oh Lord, why had he picked up?

As if he were reading the mind Louise honestly didn't know if she still possessed, F. Scott looked up. 'I answered, because I was hoping it would be you.'

'Hmmm,' said Louise, trying to stay calm. She lit a cigarette. Inhaled so hard her head began to spin. 'So?' said Louise, without exhaling. 'So?' she said, with her head and lungs still full of smoke.

'So, she said she was your best friend, which is true, right?' said F. Scott, probing. 'Missy-the-dickhead is your best friend?'

Louise exhaled. 'You got that right,' said Louise. Although soon-to-be-ex best friend was probably more like it. 'What else did she say?' Louise asked, voice squeaking.

'You're squeaking, Louise,' said F. Scott.

Louise felt her face go red and hot.

'Don't get embarrassed,' he said, embarrassing her. 'I think it's kind of cute.'

Louise took another drag. 'What else did she say?' Louise repeated herself.

'She said she was coming to New York.'

New York? Missy?

'When?' said Louise.

'I don't know,' said F. Scott. 'That was the message. She's gonna come. She's gonna come to see you. That's all I know.'

All he knows. Louise prayed that this was true. She also prayed for an air controller's strike. She prayed for the wisdom and resolve to deal with Missy's trip later.

'Okay,' said Louise. 'Message received,' she said. And then, 'But why on earth did you call her back?'

'I called her back because she said her husband was a movie director. I thought that was kind of cool.'

God, this kid was still a kid. What was a movie director but a guy who made movies and still sat around all day in his underwear, never picking up his socks?

'Yeah,' said Louise. 'So?'

'So, I was bored,' said F. Scott. 'I wanted to rent something. So I wanted to know what the guy did, so I could rent it.'

Swampeater 2? Did Missy tell him about *Swampeater 2*? Is that what she sent F. Scott Feinstadt out to the video store for? Or did she only brag about Marcos' latest blockbuster hit, a critical debacle that involved a hundred million dollars, two major box office names, a rather large boat, and the drowning death of a Polynesian stuntman?

'Okay,' said Louise. So he'd rented *Battle of the Deep*. Big deal. She could live with that.

'Okay,' said F. Scott. 'But now I've got a question.'

Louise inhaled again. 'Okay, F. Scott. What?'

He leaned in closer. He reached for her cigarette, took a drag and then ground it out on the floor with his heel. He exhaled and put his face close to hers. He put his hand on her chin. Louise had butterflies in her tummy, she had butterflies fluttering up and down her legs and arms, she had butterflies in her teeth and gums, fluttering around her soft palate. His next few words came out in a whisper.

'Would you say that Missy understands you?' asked F. Scott. 'In all the world, does Missy know you best?'

What the hell was he talking about? Louise pulled back. She reached for the cigarette pack again, but he covered her hand with his. She looked down at the bar. She decided to tell the truth now.

'Well,' said Louise, 'yes and no. I mean she knows me pretty well. She knows me as well as anybody, except for my mother maybe, except for Peter . . .'

'Shshsh,' said F. Scott. His forefinger shot through the air and rested on Louise's mouth, on her lips. He parted them. His finger played with the area where her lips suddenly turned wet and soft, where her outside met her insides, moistened satin and yielding leather. 'Let's not talk about him. This is about us only. That guy no longer exists.'

Fine by me, thought Louise.

'Missy and I have been friends for a long, long time,' she said.

This seemed to satisfy him.

They finished their sodas in silence. Then, as if he had just been stung by a bee, F. Scott hopped off of his stool and left the store, just like that. Just like that the stool next to Louise, the stool F. Scott Feinstadt had been occupying, was empty and she was alone with a bunch of giggling teenage girls slurping up their bubble sodas. Not quite sure what to do, Louise paid up, and then followed F. Scott out of the bright lights of the store and into the night. He was waiting for her on the sidewalk, a little sideways of the soda shop, in a darkened doorway.

'What's the matter with you?' Louise said when she saw him lurking in the shadows.

'I'm sorry,' said F. Scott. 'I guess I was feeling a little jealous.'

'Jealous?' said Louise. 'Of who?'

'Of anyone who knows you longer than I do. I'm jealous of every man who came before me, and any left to come. I'm the most jealous man on the planet, Louise. God. I'm even jealous of your girlfriends. I'm not a stalker, or anything, I'm just jealous.'

What the fuck is he talking about? Louise thought. Still, the tenor of his rant felt kind of sweet. F. Scott put out his hand.

He was so green. Most of the men she'd known had felt this

way, that is if they'd bothered to care at all, most men Louise knew wanted whatever woman they were seeing to only belong to them, just none of them had bothered admitting it aloud to her before.

'Forgive me?' said F. Scott.

Sure, thought Louise. Why not? It's all too confusing anyway, and I don't have anything better to do.

In silence, they walked hand in hand through the dark downtown streets. At one point F. Scott reached into his pocket and pulled out a joint, which they smoked together, passing it back and forth, as they walked. They ended up in an old Italian bar in Nolita. Marachiara. Except for three or four stock mafioso, this place was flooded with bankers and a couple of downtown old guys, guys Louise's age, guys who just one week prior she might have desperately wanted to date. Artists maybe, videographers, cool guys who were hanging out with girls even more adolescent than F. Scott was. Jailbait. Pretty girls in slip skirts and little sweaters, a pierced belly button peaking out now and then, the tiny metal loop flirting with the barroom light. But F. Scott didn't notice. He only had eyes for Louise.

At the bar, every once in a while F. Scott would cup Louise's chin with one hand, not the way he had before, not with purpose, but out of something softer now, what felt curiously like devotion. Or he would smooth some errant curl away from her face – even with all that blow-drying, her hair had frizzed up because of the heat. But when F. Scott touched her hair that way they were worth it, frizzies, they were worth paying good money for; she'd even risk a permanent or a hair weave if it meant F. Scott would keep using his long beautiful fingers to place her curls behind her ear that way. Scott Feinstadt had had long beautiful fingers. What did Peter Harrington's fingers look like? What did his hands look like? Louise could remember Scott Feinstadt's hands, those handsome fingers, the nails ringed with pigment, red and blue, black and brown, the little red scars that kissed his knuckles, the strong broad palms that took her breath away when he held them up to hers and dwarfed them, those square thick nails that studded his fingers, Scott Feinstadt's fingers encircling her bony forearm as he marveled, 'Just like a little twig I could break in half'; she remembered all of this now, the hangnails and ragged cuticles, the brown spot on his thumb – that little freckle, but Louise Harrington could not for the life of her remember the hands of her very own husband. She could not remember the hands of a man who had shared her life for over a decade. F. Scott Feinstadt's hands looked exactly like Scott Feinstadt's hands except that there were a few curly dark hairs teasing at his wrists, one or two glinting a little silver. He brushed her hair behind her ear again. Missy would die of envy, if she only knew, thought Louise, and for a minute she felt like calling her and telling her that the sweet young thing Missy had gabbed with, now couldn't stop petting her best friend Louise. But why? Louise could live some nice moment in her life without Missy's envy there to document it for her. Every once in a while, in the middle of some self-important monologue, F. Scott would look at Louise adoringly. Adoringly he would light her cigarettes, then take them from her and steal a puff. Leaning up against the bar, the cigarette smoke French-curling out from his nostrils, he looked like some slightly dissipated young movie star. A little bit of belly pushing against his T-shirt. He was a darling. And he behaved so winningly, Louise thought. She thought the word 'winningly' when she looked up into those blue eyes. She thought; win me over, motherfucker. He did. First he taught her how to play darts, and then he borrowed fifty cents from her and played the juke box. Sinatra. F. Scott grabbed Louise and twirled her around. 'This is the music for you. Good old fashioned love songs.'

When he dipped her, when all the blood and alcohol and THC accrued into a tidal rush of something amazing inside her head, she looked up at him and said: 'Honey, let's go home.'

That night, back in Louise's little apartment, they left the AC off because F. Scott said he wanted to smell her sweat. He said he wanted to taste it. It was a steamy summer night, even though it wasn't yet technically summer; it was a night that gave proof to the theory of global warming. F. Scott opened all the windows so that Louise's silken sari curtains could shimmer in the breeze. Still, he was a bit hesitant. Was he scared of her? What was there to be scared of? They'd been naked together before.

'I'm scared, Louise,' said F. Scott. 'I don't want to be another victim.'

'Of what, honey?' asked Louise.

F. Scott was trembling. Louise reached out a hand to steady him. She held his arm above his elbow.

'Of you,' F. Scott said. 'Of love.' A few tears slipped down his cheeks, but he did not brush them off.

He stood before her, so close she could feel his sweet sticky breath across her open eyes. She could smell the salt of his tears. Louise moved in closer, she pressed her lips to his wet cheeks and then she moved back and she licked them, her own lips, and his tears really did taste of the sea. She moved back in closer now and pressed her lips to his wet lashes, and when he blinked back more tears, tears just spilling out, his lashes really did feel like angel wings. She moved her lips now down his neck, resting at his pulse, where his heart beat strong and fast, and faster yet as she rested her mouth there. Everything between them felt exactly as everyone ever said it would, in the girls' bathroom at school (awkward and odiferous), in books and movies (romantic and amazing), as it had in her very own past (placing her more firmly in the moment than anything else could and yet some how lifting Louise up up up to the ceiling where she could observe the peculiarities of two bodies in motion, hers and his) and yet everything between them also felt new and different, like at last she recognized what she had always known to be true. She gasped. At the sound of that gasp, F. Scott leaned forward. He pulled her up toward him with his mouth, as if his mouth were a magnet, but also with his two strong, square hands under her rib cage, because she'd gone limp in the moment, she'd gotten wavery, as if she were viewing her own body through a veil of shimmery smoke, and he pressed her back with his mouth so that her neck arched open, and she opened him too, his teeth with her tongue, so that they were both open and moving together. F. Scott moaned, and his knees gave a little and then it was F. Scott kissing down Louise's arched neck, through her shirt, and on to her hard belly. He got down on one knee and fumbled some with her pants, until she gave in, and helped him out, and before she knew it they were going at it on her bed.

There had been a night like this one when Louise was younger. Sultry and sticky and slightly clumsy, a night like this filled with nascent, nubile love. The calisthenics involved were somewhat murky for her now – they were even murky in the very moment while similar acts were being performed with F. Scott in her adult bed, but the calisthenics of her youth were even murkier. Still, she remembered how happy she had been that night, after, when she had lain naked and damp and spent on his bed, the breeze blowing in from the gorge outside his window, the wet wet breeze, from the gorge spray, from the spray of their own bodies, who knew which, for his apartment had hung over the side of the gorge back then, like a tree house, like a stalactite, part of the rock formation. It was her favorite apartment in all of Ithaca. Her favorite apartment ever, really, because of how closely it abutted the rock wall, her favorite because of how oddly a part of nature the rickety old student house had felt. And later, after he was asleep, Louise had climbed naked onto the windowsill and smoked; she'd smoked clove cigarettes; she'd licked her lips and tasted spice, his spice, the spice of the rare Indonesian smoke that entered her lungs and took her someplace foreign and mysterious and adult, and so she smoked and smoked and looked at the rushing waterfall below, until he opened his eyes and called out to her, until he said: 'Louise, you are beautiful'; and his voice sounded more pure and honest than any voice she'd ever known, until he said, honestly and purely, 'Louise, you are the most beautiful woman in the world who isn't a movie star.'

And suddenly it had become true, she was beautiful, Louise was the most beautiful woman he had ever met, the most humanly beautiful, with all her real-life flaws that seemed to make this one young man like her even better, this one young man who had traced a path between her beauty marks, connecting the dots with his tongue, this one young man who had tenderly kissed the scar on her wrist where after her parents' divorce she had half-heartedly cut herself, this young man who thought she was the most beautiful real live woman in the world, and because he thought it, she was, she was, Louise was beautiful then, sitting and smoking in the window, her small breasts high on her rib cage, the long curly hair between her legs – so long this F. Scott was busy parting it tenderly with his gorgeous attenuated fingers, so long that in her youth Scott Feinstadt had threatened to bead and braid it – her long hair was still damp and curling between her legs, and Louise was beautiful, the most beautiful woman he'd ever met – he'd said so! – even though she didn't even think of herself as a grown woman yet, even though until that very moment, until those words had come out of his mouth, she had always thought of herself as a little girl. She had looked at him then, Scott, no not Scott, not Scott in Ithaca, Scott was dead long before she'd ever even gotten to Ithaca, no she would have had to have been looking at Peter Harrington that night, it was Peter Harrington who was invading her memories, and she'd thought then, in that moment of feeling beautiful, no one will ever love me like this again, and now in bed with F. Scott Feinstadt, Louise thought, I guess that's true. They had loved her differently, her men, but no one had ever loved her like that again, with awe; no one had run his hand down the curve of her side like it was a roller-coaster, marveling at the width of her hips, the smallness of her waist; no one had gazed that same way at her breasts, holding them all night in his hands as he slept; no one had ever not had enough of her, coming at her again and again until what was between her legs felt permanently open, a wound that would never heal. No, no one had ever loved her again, Louise Harrington, like loving her had been the very reason why he was born, until this very moment. Oh God Peter! she thought. Oh Scott. Oh F. Scott, you're either rescuing me or you're burying me. She came with a shudder in his arms.

In the morning, when Louise woke up, F. Scott was gone. She rolled over to hold him and found herself alone and wrinkled in the sticky spot. She waited awhile, showering, pouring herself a cup of coffee, not eating breakfast, thinking he'd reappear and take her out, the two of them a glowing couple with wet hair, sharing a booth at a local diner. She spent the better part of an hour straining to hear the door screech open, hoping against hope that F. Scott would present himself to her with a bag of bagels in one hand and the *New York Times* sliding out from under his arm. But no such luck. He was gone. Without a note or even a cat drawing this time. He was gone. It was hard to believe; after a night like that. But it wasn't hard to believe, either. It's not like Louise had been born yesterday. It's not like this had never happened to her before; it's not like she had never spent the same kind of crazy head-spinning evening with a boy – a boy whose conduct would lead any sane person to believe he was about to become her next boyfriend – only to find herself all alone in the morning, wretched and used and feeling cheap. She'd been around the block, Louise. She should have seen it coming. Scott Feinstadt. F. Scott Feinstadt. The fuckers were a dime a dozen. She felt like kicking herself. What was the value of all this hindsight if she wasn't going to make use of it?

She picked up the phone to call Missy. His behavior was outrageous. Louise wanted to discuss his outrageous behavior with somebody. More importantly, she wanted to know more about what had transpired between the two of them on the phone. But Missy's line rang and rang, before the oh-so-cute lisping voices of the twins came on the outgoing message. It was kind of early for Missy to be up and about, maybe she'd dropped the kids off at some new fancy form of daycare, toddler military school. Louise was just about to hang up the phone when the nanny came on.

'Hello,' said the nanny. 'Good morning.'

'Good morning, Mercedes,' said Louise. 'I hope it isn't too early for you.'

'The twins have been up since five,' said Mercedes, sighing. 'It is some job.'

Indeed.

'Is Missy there?' asked Louise.

'Missy's gone for the weekend,' said Mercedes. One of the twins began shrieking in the background. Mercedes began to hush him up in Spanish.

'Gone?' said Louise. 'Gone?'

'Cannes,' said Mercedes. 'That's where Marcos has gone.'

'Could you please give Missy a message for me? Could you tell her to call me the instant she comes home? No, wait. Tell her to call me the instant she calls you. Tell her it's an emergency, Mercedes, please.'

'Yes, yes, no,' said Mercedes. Louise couldn't tell if Mercedes was talking to her or the screaming kid.

'Mercedes?' asked Louise. But Mercedes had already hung up the phone.

So Missy had gone to Cannes. Good thing. Missy couldn't fuck with Louise's life from another continent. And Louise wasn't about to waste one more moment of self-esteem in whining on the phone. The last thing she had space for now was mooning to Missy about some guy. Unfortunately, she really didn't know what else to do with all that precious time. Of course, there was work. But then, what was work? She was the king now, she could decide if work was worth attending, she could give herself a break, a much-needed day off. She was master of her own universe. And it was Sunday morning. Sunday morning. No work anyway. Louise could go shopping. She could take in a morning movie. Check out some of the new art galleries in Chelsea. Louise dressed with purpose. She could look good. She didn't need a husband, a best friend, she didn't need a lover. She could go buy some good china for herself. Pay for her own fancy brunch.

She put a comb through her hair, packed up her shoulder bag, left a new outgoing message – 'If this is Missy, I'm in Larchmont, everyone else, please leave a message at the . . .' and took the next train home.

When Louise arrived at her mother's house, the kitchen was empty. 'Mom,' she said, 'I'm home.' But no Mom Silverstein was there to answer her. Louise walked out into the dining room, past the little den that used to be her father's study and now was something of a junk room, out into the living room, where no one had ever sat, the living room where no one had ever lived; for her entire life the living room had been saved for company.

They never had any company.

The League of Women Voters, we had the League of Women Voters.

That's not company, Mom, Louise snapped. That's a lot of well-meaning, too smart, unfulfilled divorced women.

Who else was there to invite?

Louise pondered this for a moment. Then, anybody! Anybody in the whole world, the Seltzer Man for God's sake would have been better than the League of Women Voters!

The living room with its bad art – two paintings by one of Mom's pals during her 'rage' stage, some folk art, a couple of framed prints from the Metropolitan Museum of Art, a family portrait that Sammy had painted in first grade of Mom, Dad and Sammy, Louise pointedly left out, which had delighted Mom, *it was so healthy and expressive!*, the living room with its yellow rugs, with its long curving green sectional sofa, parked in the middle of the room like a dead snake. The living room was as bereft of living as it had ever been.

'Mom,' called Louise.

Where was she? It had never occurred to Louise that she could arrive at home with no Mom Silverstein waiting there to greet her.

Panic began to rise in her throat.

'Mom, Mom!' Louise called out. 'Mommy, where are you?'

She headed upstairs, stumbling a little on the Oriental runner that should have been tacked down more securely – her mother could trip and break her neck – up to the second story of Mom's faux Colonial.

'Mom,' called Louise.

She pushed open the door to her old bedroom first, no Mom, the bathroom down the hall, no. With fear in her heart – why wasn't Mom answering her? – Louise saw that her mother's bedroom door was open, and she headed for it, calling 'Mom, Mom,' as she got closer and closer.

Mom was lying on her bed. Old and gray. Oddly tiny in the moment, curled up on the ripped and worn patchwork spread, like a little bird, like a plump little bird who had fallen out of the nest. Stunned, and beginning to worry. Her eyes were fluttering open. Where am I? Mom's eyes said. What world is this? How will I survive here? Louise had never seen this expression on Mom's face before, although the sentiment was one that she herself felt almost daily.

'Louise?' Mom said. As if she weren't quite sure who Louise was. Then her face, Mom's old, familiar face, began to take shape. 'I was just taking a little rest.'

A little rest, in the middle of the day. What a thought, Mom resting.

'Oh Mom,' said Louise, relief flooding through her.

'What's wrong, honey?' said Mom.

'Oh, I don't know. Everything? Peter, Mom. Peter and this new guy I met.'

Her mother opened up her arms. Her grown daughter climbed onto the bed and let her suddenly elderly mother wrap those same arms around her.

'He's got a new girlfriend, Peter,' Louise said.

'I'm glad you're home,' said Mom.

Louise was, too; she was glad she was home, lying in her parents' old double bed with her Mom.

Her spitfire, pain-in-the-ass, constantly commenting mother. Louise loved her.

'He's got a new girlfriend, Mom,' Louise said again. This time her voice broke. 'Can you believe it?'

Mom patted Louise's head. Even her hand through Louise's hair felt birdlike and frail.

'Yes, darling, I can,' said Mom. And then, as if to herself, 'I'm so glad I'm not young. I'm so glad I'll never ever have to be young again.'

Louise spent most of the afternoon and evening talking with Mom. Not about Peter, not about what's-his-name; they talked on and on about the house, about Hillary Clinton, about Sammy some, about Mom herself when her Mom had been a girl. After that initial comfort session on the bed, Louise had decided to spare her, she'd decided to let Mom have a little rest. And in a way, it was enough, it was enough just to be by Mom, it was enough to just physically occupy the same space with her, which seemed to stop Mom from constantly nattering inside Louise's head. In fact, in the present, in the flesh, at least at first, Mom seemed oddly content not to natter at all, not to pry. In the flesh, Mom seemed happy not to know the whole story. Maybe even Mom had her own problems, maybe even Mom finally had enough. So Louise spared her. They ordered Chinese and Louise drove to the restaurant to pick it up. Then when Mom went to bed, Louise stayed on and did the dishes, dropping a plastic chopstick down into the dishwasher's well, and wrenching her neck in a good way during the process of freeing it. *In a good way?* It cracked, Mom . . . So in relation to proximity, the nattering seemed to stop when Mom was awake and could do it live and in person.

In the morning, after Louise hadn't called in sick – she was king, she reminded herself, she was the acting admissions coordinator! – mother and daughter went shopping together at Loehmann's. It was in the Back Room, with the designer fashions, the labels cut out but still leaving bold hints as to their sartorial origins: Ca—lein, —ada, Ral—uren, that Mom showed some of her old private investigator spunk. She was flipping through a rack of Tahari (Ta–ri) sleeveless suits for Louise, in a bluish bullet gray, when the subject of the Feinstadts came up. Mom said, 'I saw Fran Horowitz the other day at the Cheese Bazaar, and so I asked her what the Feinstadts were up to.' Mom's eyes never left the rack as she talked. But she paused here in her conversation, waiting for Louise to tip her hand, show interest. Louise decided to accommodate her.

'I never requested it, Mom, I just . . . I . . .,' she stopped to catch her breath.

'And . . .,' said Louise.

'And,' said Mom, 'apparently the rabbi went loopy about half a year ago. He quit his congregation, cashed in his retirement and bought a boat, took off before Rachel got wind of any of it. She woke up one morning and found herself husbandless, penniless and futureless. She's now in law school in Gainesville. Her son-in-law is paying for it. The rabbi, that nut, he's been sailing the Caribbean ever since, at least that's what Fran thinks. He keeps in touch with the girls from time to time, can you believe it? Sometimes he asks for money, but they don't like to tell their mother much, they're afraid to get caught in the middle. What middle? This is a story without a middle ground.'

Mom moved from the blue to the olive drab suits, one rack over. She was barely breathing. Louise would have been completely winded after such a verbal eruption; in fact, she herself was breathing heavily – the old hyperventilation – but Mom hadn't even broken an anaerobic sweat. Louise followed her from one rack to the other.

'You're kidding, Mom. Poor Mrs Feinstadt. That's awful. But he's a rabbi. A rabbi wouldn't do such a thing.'

'What's a rabbi?' said Mom. 'A rabbi is still a man.'

Louise remembered Scott Feinstadt's father. As rabbis go he had been kind of dashing, as dashing as a middle-aged rabbi could be with a Larchmont congregation. She remembered how he had let Scott use the synagogue basement for his studio. She remembered how he had sat through Scott's funeral with one teardrop dangling from his nose. She remembered resisting the urge to take her own balled-up Kleenex and reach out to wipe it.

'Apparently he had a breakdown,' Mom said, not able to stand the silence.

'She had no warning?' asked Louise.

'Warning?' said Mom. 'In hindsight with these things there's always warning.' Here she took a suit off the rack and held it up against Louise. It was a maneuver designed to catch Louise unaware and hold her with Mom's eyes. Which she did, she held Louise with her eyes.

'Right, honey? When a marriage breaks up, with hindsight there is always writing on the wall. Am I right?'

Louise nodded.

Mom moved the suit away. 'I don't think this would do much for your hips,' Mom said. She turned back to the rack. 'According to Fran, the psychiatrist Rachel consulted said that this was a case of post-traumatic stress syndrome. He felt that the boy's death had finally caught up to him, the rabbi, I mean. He said it could have happened to anyone who didn't properly deal with their grief at the time. Apparently, a few weeks before he cracked up the rabbi had told Annie that Scott had showed up at the temple looking for a job. Back from the dead. Still nineteen or twenty, whatever that poor kid was. He comes back as a rabbinical student, yet. That wild child. And Annie didn't think her father needed professional help? Scott shows up bearded. In payos, the rabbi said. He called himself Simcha, for God's sake. And Annie, that idiot, didn't tell anyone.' Her Mom held another style up against Louise, and sighed. 'It was as if Irv Feinstadt had taken out an ad in the newspaper – "I'm having a psychotic episode."'

'What?' said Louise.

'It was a Reform shul,' said Mom, and she rolled her finger near her temple. 'Payos? Right.'

'What are you talking about, Scott showed up?' Louise said, heart racing.

'Look, some kid came knocking, that's all. The rabbi was obviously nuts.'

'Nuts?'

'Certifiable,' said Mom. 'It's best to deal with problems as they arise, Louise. Do you understand what I'm saying?'

Louise nodded yes, although she wasn't sure.

'Is this what you were looking for?' Mom held the suit up closer to Louise.

Louise nodded. The suit looked like it would fit her perfectly.

'I bet your new young man might like this, honey,' her Mom said.

'There is no new young man,' Louise said, because it was true. Her young man was recycled. And neither he nor her old man had bothered to call. She'd checked her answering machine when she told Mom she was going to the ladies' room.

'The old one will like it, too,' Mom said, and she moved on to the D—Y.

After Loehmann's, Louise helped Mom pick up the flats of pansies and impatiens she had ordered at the nursery, and then Louise left Mom in the yard, ostensibly to go to the bathroom again. But once alone in her mother's kitchen, Louise picked up the phone, using her own phone card to call information and make the long-distance call. She called F. Scott Feinstadt at his mother's house on Long Island from her mother's house in Larchmont, a mother-to-mother call, keeping an eye out the kitchen window on her own Mom working in the yard. The phone rang three times before a woman picked up.

'Mrs Feinstadt?' said Louise, sotto voce.

'Hello? Hello?' said the woman on the other end of the line. 'You'll have to speak up, I can't hear you.'

'I'm looking for F. Scott Feinstadt,' Louise said, in the equivalent of a stage whisper.

'He's at Ricky's,' said Mrs Feinstadt.

Ricky's. Isn't that where he always told his mother he was staying when he was staying with some girl?

And then, Mrs Feinstadt said: 'Who is this, please?'

'Do you have the number?' said Louise.

'It's somewhere in the City,' said Mrs Feinstadt, and then, more firmly, 'Whom should I say is calling?'

'Louise?' called Mom from the yard.

'Louise,' Louise breathed into the phone.

'Louise?' said Mrs Feinstadt.

In a panic, Louise hung up the phone. She hung up on F. Scott's mother.

Her hands were shaking. This was not the first time she had hung up on someone's mother. She used to call Scott Feinstadt's home, maybe three, four times a day, hoping he would pick up, which he never did, he was too cool back then to answer the phone, and she would inevitably hang up on Mrs Feinstadt.

'I'll be there in a moment, Mom,' Louise called out into the yard. And then she quickly dialed information. 'Margarita Cipriani,' Louise breathed into the phone. But at the request of the customer, the number was unlisted.

'Louise,' called Mom, 'did you fall in?' and on that note, Louise hung up the phone and stumbled out into the yard. There they fought a little about the future of Medicare and Social Security while Louise helped Mom turn over the flower beds. She was herself, Mom, still 'the little spitfire in a pantsuit', but a little bit littler now – osteoporosis – and ever a little bit less spitfiery. She had to sit every so often, Mom, she had to rest – they were officially in a verifiable heat wave, they'd said so on NPR, and the humidity was worse – the veins in Mom's hands and arms looked like blue worms that could wriggle right off when she dug her way through the dirt. Part of Louise wanted to confess it all, the hang-ups, Scott, F. Scott, sex fiend Peter, and part of her didn't feel like providing Mom with ammunition. Mom had thought the rabbi was nuts, what would she make of her own daughter? Had F. Scott first flown down to Florida before coming up north to haunt her, or was he peopling the earth like *Night of the Living Dead?* Were Rabbi Feinstadt and Louise both suffering from the same disorder? Would it kill Mom to learn that Louise was totally off her rocker? No. Louise wasn't totally off her rocker. F. Scott Feinstadt hadn't come to her with payos. But perhaps Louise and the rabbi had both fashioned their very own brand of visitation – he'd come as they each wanted him to be.

Louise shared none of this with Mom. She kept her mouth shut for the rest of her visit. And at the end of the day, she walked her mother upstairs. While she waited for her to emerge from the master bath, Louise thought she heard the portable phone ring downstairs, but before she could run and answer it, her mom emerged in an old flannel nightgown, looking rather like a child. Louise showed her how to work the TV clicker for the thousandth time and then tucked her into bed. Then Louise repacked her own bag, threw on her cardigan and headed downstairs.

Sammy, her brother, was sitting in the kitchen. He was at the table eating a nice piece of store-bought pie. Out of the box, still in its little silver plate. The pie was boysenberry. Louise knew this because Sammy's teeth flashed purple and boysenberry had always been his favorite – what else would Mom Silverstein buy?

Louise's favorite?

I didn't know you were coming.

Did you know Sammy was coming? He didn't even announce himself when he arrived.

Why should he announce himself? It's his house. Sammy always drops by to see his mother. So I keep a little something handy for him, in the bread box.

Well, you should have bought my favorite pie just in case, thought Louise, to keep handy in the bread box. You should have bought it because you wanted me to stop by. To will me back here.

You don't eat pie, Louise.

This stumped her.

At least not in public.

Thank you, Mom.

'Louise,' said Sammy. 'How the hell are you?'

Even though he'd barely looked up from his pie, Sammy's voice had all the joviality of a Wall Street broker's and it cut through her reverie the same way such a person might cut through the crowds at Times Square to make his train. With a jolly disregard for anyone else. Which made sense, since a Wall Street broker was what Sammy was. At least as far as Louise could figure. He was a deal-maker, her brother. With an expense account, but without a soul. Louise half-expected him to slap her on the shoulder.

It took every ounce of effort that she could muster for Louise to keep her cool. 'Hey, Sammy. I'm fine. And you?'

'Golden,' said Sammy, and he continued eating. He was reading the *Wall Street Journal, Sports Illustrated* and *New York* magazine all at the same time. Sammy had always read periodicals the same way he watched television – he channel-surfed.

The poor kid has ADD. That's why he got into drugs, he was self-medicating.

He was a nice-looking man, for a drug addict, for a traitor, Sammy, with his corporate buzz cut, Armani glasses shaped like a Stingray's fender, like something their very own father might have worn in the '50s, with his white, white, ultra-white T-shirt – How did he get them so white? *He must use bleach. He must wear them once, Ma, and throw them out. No, he sends them out for dry-cleaning.* They're too perfect, Ma, they're too blindingly, blisteringly white. *People are starving in China, they're starving in Red Hook.* He still throws them out. *Not Sammy, Sammy gives more to charity than you and I make in a year* – his strong jaw, big brown eyes, with lashes that still tickled the back of his lids. *He was such a beautiful baby!* He looked like what he was, a rich guy on his day off hanging out in the kitchen of his mother. He looked like a stranger, like a guy who two decades prior might have sported a pinkie ring, but now in the midst of the millennium just tooled around in Gucci; he looked like someone Louise would never ever know.

She took off her sweater, pulled out the chair next to Sammy and sat down at the table. She and Sammy had sat like this many times at the table in the kitchen of their ancestral home. They had breakfasted together, the Cap'n Crunch box standing like a wall between them, each happy to block out the sight of the other. They had eaten their snacks together, after school, Louise cutting up her favorite fruit into tinier and tinier pieces so that they would last longer, Sammy eating a Nestlé's Thousand Dollar bar/peanut-butter sandwich melt. So many times they had found each other in this same spot when they'd both sneaked down to eat leftovers after Thanksgiving, or to break into the liquor cabinet on a trip home for the High Holy Days, or even back in junior high and high school to smoke some pot, the oven fan on, the windows open, the joint passing back and forth between them, the smoke a helix, a piece of DNA linking them in the only way they could possibly be linked, genetically, and through their mutual desire for obliteration. A million, zillion times, Louise and her baby brother had sat this same way at this same table, but they'd never really had a conversation, had they, Louise and Sammy? They'd always sat in some variation of silence, variations that consisted of asking the other about their health, education and welfare, a grunt or two about the state of their aging parents, silence after all.

Not this day. Not if Louise could help it. This day was going to be different. Louise was changing. She had to. What a tragedy it would be to just grow older, for adults just to be taller, harder, more wrinkled kids.

'How could you?' said Louise, her voice trembling a little. And then, 'Sammy, you're my brother.'

'What?' said Sammy, as he gulped down his final swallow.

'My brother, my brother,' Louise repeated, and in the repetition the words sounded like an incantation.

'I know I'm your brother,' said Sammy. Did he know what being a brother meant? 'How could I what?'

It took Louise a moment to answer. A moment to still her beating heart.

'Peter,' said Louise, and a tear or two slipped down her face; she caught them with her fingers.

'You're gonna cry now?' said Sammy. And then, a bit softer, 'Don't cry. It's not so bad, he's doing better, the poor guy's doing really good . . .'

'You could have told me,' said Louise.

'He asked me not to. So, no, Louise, I could not have.'

Even Sammy, in the moment, had some dignity, when he was saying it, without a contraction. Could not have! Louise didn't. Dignity had never been her middle name. Why in the weeks that followed Scott Feinstadt's breaking up with her, even after she learned that he had gone on to date Missy, Louise's best friend, she'd had no dignity, *sweetie, you groveled in the dirt.* It was true, she had, she'd made him a tape of all their songs and sneaked it into the boom box he kept in the front seat of the red truck because he couldn't afford a car stereo, in the hopes of reminding him of her. She'd written him letters, some of which she'd actually sent; she remembered one she'd penned in calligraphy on rice paper, a little sexy haiku: 'Sweet strawberry juice . . .' Oh, God, it hurt so much now to remember. If there were a bedsheet around anywhere, even in her mother's kitchen, she would have pulled it up to cover her head. No. Dignity. Dignity was in order. She knew more now. She could handle it. Even Sammy had dignity. She hated his fucking guts.

'Okay,' said Louise. 'I respect that. I really do. He asked you to keep mum, so you did. But still, not to at least have hinted . . . I'm your sister. That was stupid.' Louise's voice was rising now, Louise's voice was taking wing.

'It's not stupid, Louise. It could make us all a lot of money. And money is not a stupid thing,' Sammy rose up from his chair to leave.

'Money? Money? Who cares about goddamn money!'

'I do,' said Sammy. 'And so do a lot of other people.'

'I'm not talking about the money, Sammy. Although of course I should be, trying to fleece Peter for God's sake . . .'

'Fleece him? I'm trying to make him rich!'

'I'm not talking about that, you asshole. Aren't you every going to listen? I'm talking about, you know . . . Everything.'

Sammy looked at her. He looked at the table. He looked at Louise again.

'I already explained it to you,' said Sammy. 'Peter spoke to me in confidence. It was not my job to be the one to tell you what you should already have known.'

Tears stung Louise's eyes. Her body was trembling. She looked at Sammy and he looked at her.

'Excuse me, if I think it was,' said Louise.

'Grow up, already, why don't you,' said Sammy. Then he got up and headed for the door.

'Sammy,' she called. 'Aren't you at least going to say goodbye to Mom?'

'She's asleep, right?' said Sammy. 'I just swung by for a little dessert.'

He walked towards the back door, his fingers on the knob.

'Oh, by the way, I almost forgot, while you were upstairs with Mom, Marcos called.'

'Marcos?'

'Yeah, Marcos.'

'Why would Marcos call me here?' Louise mused. Why would he call her period?

'He was looking for Missy. He seems to think she's staying with you. Or something like that, the connection was bad. I think he said he was in Cannes. Is there some high-budget bomb category for him to compete in now?'

Sammy harrumphed at his own little quip – he hated Hollywood, thought those bozos got rich just by doing lunch – and then he turned the knob and opened the back door.

'Sammy, why would Marcos think Missy was staying with me?'

'How the hell should I know, Louise,' he said. 'You figure it out.' And then he stepped out of the house, out of her life.

'Sammy, you motherfucker . . .'

Louise heard the door slam. Marcos thought that Missy was staying with her. In New York? Had to be, Missy hated Larchmont. There was that outgoing message on Louise's answering machine. Sammy said it was not his job . . . that she should have already known. Why hadn't she known? Why hadn't she known her very own husband? Did anyone ever really know anyone? Marcos thought that Missy was in New York. Sammy said, figure it out.

For the first time in Louise's life, she decided to listen to Sammy.

F. Scott. F. Scott and Missy had talked on the phone. Marcos thought Missy was with her. F. Scott had said Missy was coming to New York.

This time Louise would figure it out. The writing was on the wall. If F. Scott was missing, then Missy must have found him.

———◆———

Louise ran all the way to the train station. She caught the very next train just as the doors were about to close. When she reached Grand Central Station, she ran to a stand of pay phones, side-stepping a sleeping derelict, and dialed up her own number, just to see if Missy had left her any messages, if Peter or F. Scott had deigned to call, but the tape came up empty. Louise brushed the hair out of her eyes. It was late and she was tired and sort of sweaty, but she wasn't ready to go home. She could call California again, but what could Mercedes tell her now that she hadn't told her the other morning? She could try to track Marcos down in Cannes, but that felt like a losing proposition, especially when the poor guy was wasting his own dime trying to track his errant wife down in Larchmont. She decided to call all the hotels in the area that Missy and Marcos liked to frequent in the hopes of finding Missy herself. The Four Seasons, The Mark, The Carlyle, where as it turned out, Missy was registered under her own name.

Sloppy, sloppy.

With a thunking heart and sweaty palms, Louise asked the operator to connect her.

The phone picked up on the second ring.

Missy.

That little bitch.

'Hi, Miss,' said Louise. 'It's me.'

There was silence on the line. It took Missy several moments to finally answer her.

'How did you find me?' said Missy.

'Marcos called me at my mother's. He was looking for you.'

'You didn't tell him where I was, did you?' asked Missy.

'I didn't know where you were, Missy,' said Louise. 'But no, you're in luck, I didn't speak to him. Sammy answered the phone.'

'Sammy,' said Missy. 'I owe the bastard a call. He's advising me on some investments. I forget, did I even bother to tell you?'

No.

'Sink all your dough into whatever it is,' said Louise. 'Sink the kids' college tuition. Whatever he says, it's a sure bet, a sure thing.' Louise would eke out her revenge. 'That's my best advice, Missy. Truly.'

Missy sighed audibly over phone. She wasn't stupid.

'Look, before we start shedding blood over this thing, why don't you hop in a cab and come on over?' said Missy.

Louise took the subway. It was hotter than hell inside the tunnel. When she got off at seventy-seventh street and Lexington Avenue she was right across the street from Lenox Hill Hospital, where her father had worked for thirty years. Thirty years and Louise had never even seen his office. After the subway, the night air felt cool and wet. She shivered as it dried the perspiration that had been beading on her neck. She walked quickly to the Carlyle.

When Louise arrived at Missy's suite – predictably over-done, drapey, carpeted gold, upholstered blue – Missy was curled up on a loveseat in the living room.

She was looking really great.

Despite herself, Louise had to comment on that fact, disheveled Louise, Louise who had been running like a maniac, she had to tell the truth.

'You look great, Miss,' said Louise.

'Fake tan, botox, water bra, good genes,' said Missy.

Louise sat down, awestruck in a chair. Missy had her feet up on another chair, her legs spread out, drinking a margarita. A hotel blender sat sweating on the coffee table. It would leave a ring, but Louise knew Missy didn't care. Why should she? It wasn't hers.

She was Louise's best friend.

You never learn.

For a moment, Louise tried to convince herself that Missy had come all the way to New York because she knew Louise was in trouble, she knew Louise, Missy, she knew her 'better than anyone', she sensed Louise had something brewing and Missy wanted to come to her rescue. With Missy there, Louise wouldn't have to face it all alone. The time warp was complete now; Louise was quoting Janis Joplin, who had already been dead ten years when Louise had copied all the lyrics to 'Bobby McGee' first on her blue jean skirt and then her social studies notebook. Still, Louise wasted the next few moments lying to herself.

When she couldn't take it any longer: 'Marcos called,' said Louise. 'He thinks you're staying with me. Are you? 'Cause if you are, it would only be right to inform me, don't you think.'

'Oh, who gives a shit about Marcos,' said Missy. 'I saw him, Wheezy,' said Missy. Her eyes glowed like a cat's. Her face seemed lit from within. 'I saw him.'

So it was true. Louise's stomach dropped. She felt like she had to go to the bathroom.

'You were holding out on me, baby-doll. You know you shouldn't do that.' Missy sounded like a mafioso.

'Saw who?' said Louise. Stalling for time, acting on instinct.

'You know who,' said Missy. 'Feinstadt. I saw him.'

If she'd seen him, it meant that he really existed, right? It meant he wasn't a figment of Louise's imagination. It meant that he was real.

'He's real,' said Louise. It was a statement, but she said it like a question. She said it with surprise. In wonderment.

'He's real,' said Missy. 'He's him.'

Even though Missy's sentence scared her, even though everything about the situation scared her, for a moment Louise didn't feel alone. She was with her best friend; and her best friend knew her biggest secret. Her best friend understood.

'I can't believe he's real,' said Louise, and her whole body began to shake. 'I can't believe I'm not crazy.'

'You're shaking, Louise,' said Missy. She put out her hand, took Louise's hand to steady her. 'Don't shake.' And then, with a little laugh, 'Just because he's real, it doesn't mean you're not crazy. Ha, ha. Although if you're crazy, I guess it means I'm crazy too. Maybe we're having a synchronized acid flashback. You know what they say about girlfriends and their periods. Maybe we're having synchronized nervous breakdowns.'

It was hard for Louise to breathe, but it helped to have Missy's hand on hers, it helped to have Missy joking, to have her best friend onboard.

'It's all pretty fucking weird, don't you think?' Louise was crying now, with relief, with awe. The whole situation had gotten to her; it was scaring her, that her secret was out now, that against all odds, what she hoped and prayed for had turned out to be true. Scott Feinstadt was back; Missy had seen him too.

'Weird, shmeird,' said Missy. 'That's life. The question is, what are we going to do?'

———◆———

With some ice, tequila, triple sec, some fancy lime juice that Missy had brought all the way from the Farmer's Market in

L.A. in her old Kate Spade diaper bag (as if they didn't have adequate lime juice in New York; 'Trust me, Wheezy, you don't') plus a ring of bitter salt, Missy whipped up another batch of margaritas in the hotel's fancy blender, and the two of them drank heartily, Missy stripping down in the process. In this expensive hotel the air-conditioning was hardly working, not like in Louise's pad, Louise thought triumphantly, but Louise kind of liked the tenor of the air in Missy's suite, she liked that it was steamy. She was lounging in one of Peter's old button-downs she'd gotten from the closet at her mother's, and Missy was in a pair of Marcos' old boxers and said water bra. They smoked cigarettes and drank, the margaritas going down like lemonade, lubricating their talk.

'You must have died when you first saw him,' said Missy. Confiding now. Close.

'I couldn't believe my eyes. But then again, I could,' said Louise. 'It was as if I never actually believed he was dead. Does anybody ever believe anyone is dead, really? Don't you always feel like they just moved to another town?'

'I believe they're dead,' said Missy, using one hand to tie her curly hair up into a knot. 'I just don't ever believe that they'll stay dead,' said Missy.

Louise stretched out her legs. She sat up. That was it, that was it exactly. She'd only believed Scott Feinstadt would stay dead for a while. Maybe that's why he'd made his way back to her. Missy understood. She got it.

'Un-hunh,' said Louise. 'I was surprised to see him, but it also kind of made sense, it kind of made sense to have him around.'

Missy nodded in agreement. Her hair knot tumbled down. She reached for her drink, and after sipping deeply she used the sweat from the icy cold glass to wet her fingers. She ran them through her hair, to tame her curls, but she only succeeded in looking more and more like a wild child when she did this.

'He looks good, hunh?' said Missy. 'Better than I would have predicted.' Both of her hands were working hard now, grabbing and bunching, determinedly reknotting her hair. 'I mean, it's true I never thought he would be balding so early, but . . . his dad wasn't bald, was he?'

They were girlfriends now. Talking, confiding, trusting in one another. 'It's one of those things that gets passed down by the mother,' said Louise, taking a swig from her own margarita. 'The male pattern baldness gene.' Peter had told her that. Peter had told her that, early on when they were contemplating having children of their own. Unfortunately, Louise's father was a cueball. Peter had said this lightly; it was one of his many excuses for not wanting kids. 'Let's go for the latex tonight,' said Peter, which was kind of sweet in the moment, because Louise hated her diaphragm and her doctor had advised her to go off the Pill, although now knowing what she knew, going for the latex must have been part of Peter's MO.

'Was Mrs Feinstadt's father bald?' asked Missy, lighting up another cigarette.

'Who knows? I think he died in Dachau.'

'Well, that's a downer,' said Missy. 'Let's focus on the boy.'

Focus on the boy. Focus on the boy. Focusing on the boy;

that felt good. It was good for Louise to have someone to do all that focusing with, to talk to. It was good to learn that she wasn't insane, or at least if she was, that she was part of a collective insanity. Collective unconscious? The term had never made sense to Louise before.

'How did you find him, Missy?' Louise asked.

Missy was eager to tell. To brag. To show off her detective work. As had already been established, Missy had called Louise's apartment while Louise was at the office.

'For heaven's sake, why?' said Louise.

'I forget sometimes,' said Missy. 'I forget you have a place to go to. You're the only person I know with a regular job.'

So when she'd called, she'd gotten F. Scott on the telephone. Louise knew this, she knew that they had spoken, F. Scott had told her, but it hadn't really sunk in that he and Missy had actually *talked* talked.

Actually, they'd had a long conversation that day – 'a regular gabfest', said Missy – F. Scott pumping Missy for information on Louise, Missy trying to figure out who this mysterious boy was.

His voice had given him away.

'Oh, not just his voice,' said Missy, blowing smoke rings into the air, but what he said, the words he used to say it. 'It was like déjà vu all over again,' said Missy. 'I felt like I was myself with him, the one I forgot about, well not exactly myself, not my relaxed sweatpants-at-home-eating-peanut-butter-out-of-the-jar-hairy-armpit self, but the girl part. You know. I felt like I recognized my face in the mirror and it was a girl's face, my face, the face of me as a girl. It wasn't the face that belonged to somebody's mother.'

The girl face. That was it exactly. That was how F. Scott had made Louise feel. Like she had her girl face back on. Trust Missy to put her finger on it.

But it wasn't until about a half an hour into her conversation with F. Scott – half an hour! – that Missy had thought to ask this mystery man his name. Missy had talked with Louise's boyfriend for a half an hour? *A leopard doesn't change his spots, Louisey.* Mom must have been waking from a dream.

'I had him repeat himself three times, and then I made the poor kid spell it out,' said Missy. 'He must have thought I was crazy.'

Crazy like a fox, thought Louise. But she held her tongue here. There was more information she wanted to glean.

Since then, Missy had spoken to F. Scott a lot. In the aggregate, it sounded like she'd spoken to him more than Louise had in the short time that she'd known him, in the short time that F. Scott had changed everything, rocked her world. When Missy couldn't take it any more – 'I fucking couldn't take it any more,' said Missy – when she felt for sure she was losing her mind, Missy had dumped the kids with the nanny – Marcos was busy diving off the Miramax yacht in Cannes – bought a full-priced ticket (Missy could do that) and headed for the coast to view him in the flesh. This coast. JFK. She'd had F. Scott meet her at her hotel. That was two days ago, said Missy. Two mother fucking days. Just when F. Scott had gone AWOL on Louise. At the crack of dawn, he'd left her sleeping alone in her apartment so that he could eat egg-white omelettes with Missy at $22.50 a pop. The carrot in all this? Missy would fill him in on the mysteries of Louise. He was curious about her, Missy said. It was like he was on some fact-finding mission.

'I mean, if you were a kid, wouldn't you want to know all you could about the divorced older lady you were boinking?'

Bitch, thought Louise. When a boy came into the mix, they weren't girlfriends any longer. Hadn't it always been this way? No wonder Louise hadn't heard from him. The past two days were Missy time, while stupid Louise had been in Larchmont watching her mother age. For the past two days Missy had been making the moves, doing her Missy thing, taking him to lunch, an art gallery . . . She was fucking bribing him, thought Louise; disparaging her . . . 'I told him the truth about your marriage,' said Missy. 'I took him to the Gap and bought him socks . . .'

Louise couldn't take it any longer. 'What truth about my marriage?'

'That it wasn't a marriage,' said Missy. 'I know, I'm the one who took your midnight phone calls over that last God-knows-how-many years.'

'Who are you to judge what a marriage is?' said Louise. 'You and Marcos and your silly games. We lived together, we loved each other, we held each other's head when we vomited.'

'Look, everyone knows Peter's a great guy. So? So then why did you opt out?'

Why? Why. Who knew why in the moment? Because Peter was fucking boring? Because Peter was fucking everything? Because she hadn't realized he was fucking everything, that he was in trouble, that he was sick, that he was trying to protect her from whatever it was that was wrong with him?

Because, let's face it, intimacy does breed contempt.

Louise was dizzy.

'The fact is that all your men meet a bad end,' said Missy. 'Peter, Wheezy, Scott . . .'

'You didn't tell him about Scott?'

'Excuse me. I'm not an idiot,' said Missy. 'I told him about some old lover; I wasn't stupid enough to say his stupid name.'

It wasn't clear from the conversation just exactly how much progress Missy had made.

'Just exactly how much progress did you make, Miss?' said Louise.

'Not enough, but enough,' said Missy.

Louise sipped her drink.

'I touched him.'

'You touched him?' said Louise.

'You better believe it, sister,' said Missy. 'I touched that creamy skin.'

Missy's eyes were flashing. She was excited, animated, drunk, mad. Louise had never seen Missy this mad before. Or this nasty. Not since the cruel, sexy, heady days of their youth back in Larchmont. Missy had been nasty and Louise had had no dignity. One of the letters Louise had sent to Scott Feinstadt after he dumped her had said, 'I would be open to a part-time relationship.' A part-time relationship? Where in the hell had Louise picked up that phrase? Why hadn't she called a spade a spade? I'll be your girl on the side, she should have said, I'll be your goddamn mistress. After the letter was sent – there was no taking it back, try as she might to fit her hand all the way down the mouth of the mailbox – Louise had been cornered by Missy and Scott and two 'impartial' friends at the Cheese Bazaar. Scott had shown Missy the letter – Louise guessed hopefully that some of its contents must have appealed to him – and Missy decided that the matter had to be handled once and for all, by and for all of them.

Oh God, it was hard to remember, the pain, the humiliation. The five teenagers had sat down cross-legged on the loading dock during one of Scott Feinstadt's half-hour breaks. The tribunal – Allison Harris and Lori Bookerman – were there to keep the meeting fair. It was decided, after much discussion, that Scott could still see Louise, but they weren't allowed to fuck. 'See' her? What did that mean? Louise had hoped it meant that they were permitted to kiss; she didn't dare ask for clarification. But after their first date, after said arrangement, Missy put her foot down. They'd gone to a movie, no kisses, no kisses when he'd brought her home, how Louise's mouth ached, she hadn't had any idea what to do with her hands. Scott Feinstadt was sitting next to her in the movie theater, hunched forward the way he always hunched, so adorably, his back so invitingly strokable, that Louise had had to sit out the whole flick on her thumbs. Missy had made Scott break up with Louise, again. That very night, Scott had called Louise when her back door had hardly finished slamming, and said: 'Missy says this isn't working.' He'd called her on the telephone from Missy's house. He'd gone to Missy's house after their date! Louise could hear Missy breathing on the extension. As Louise remembered it now – she'd conveniently forgotten this part over the years, this messy back-and-forth, embarrassing, horribly humiliating part – Scott Feinstadt had broken up twice with her that summer, and she hadn't seen him alone again until the morning he gave her that painting, a few days before he headed up to the Rhode Island School of Design. End of story.

That was high school in a nutshell, that tribunal. It had been horrible even before Scott Feinstadt died. In fact, while he was alive, everything had been worse.

'How could you hold out on me?' said Missy. 'I loved him too.' Louise was surprised by her intensity. It was a cri de coeur. Missy felt betrayed by her.

This time, for the first time, Missy felt that she was the one who had been betrayed.

Not Louise; she was used to a friend betraying her. She was weaned on that feeling. So now, it was Missy's turn. Missy, who suddenly was into sharing. It was a little late for that.

'I understand,' said Louise, tipping back her drink. 'But who cares?'

Missy stared at her. This *was* a new Louise.

'It wouldn't work,' said Louise, quoting Missy back to Missy. 'Sharing him with you.'

Missy gulped, loudly. Clearly, she hadn't expected this.

Emboldened, Louise said, 'He's mine now, Miss. That's all that matters. Possession is nine-tenths of the law. I'm the one he wants.'

Again, there was silence in the room.

'What? So that's it? He's yours? But who the hell is he?' said Missy. 'You think he's come back from the dead?'

'Don't you?' said Louise. 'You just said . . . you said it was him.'

'I said it was him, sure it's him, who else would it be? But you know you have to be a little nuts to think it's him, him.'

'You said it was him, him,' said Louise. 'You just said it.'

Missy laughed out loud. 'What, now you believe in reincarnation, Louise? A little mojo, wooh-wooh, what the fuck? I mean, sure it looks like him, I believe it's him, but I don't believe it, I mean, it can't be him, you can't believe it's him, him, do you, Louise? Are you nuts? Do you think I'm nuts, like you?'

Louise shook her head; she didn't know. She didn't care. Missy was just trying to confuse her.

'I don't care,' Louise said.

'You don't care?' said Missy.

'No,' said Louise, 'I don't. I've got him and I want him. He belongs to me.'

'He was mine when he died,' said Missy.

'I don't care,' said Louise.

'He was mine when he died,' said Missy. Threateningly.

'Yeah, well,' said Louise. 'So what? So what? If he had lived maybe he would have come back to me.'

Missy shook her head. Her eyes narrowed.

'He'd decided already, Louise. It was over.'

'If he had lived long enough he would have missed me,' Louise said. 'He would have seen you for what you are.'

'Which is what?' said Missy.

'A dickhead!' said Louise.

'That's mature,' said Missy.

'If he had lived, he would have dumped you for some shiksa goddess millinery major!'

'If he had lived, maybe we would have gotten married, had some kids and lived in Soho . . .'

'Maybe he would have ended up working for his uncle's car dealership in Jersey.'

Missy smiled a wicked smile.

'Jealous?' said Missy.

'Jealous of what?' said Louise.

'Jealous that me and my artist husband and our gorgeous children and Jack Russell terrier live in Soho?'

'You're out of your mind, Miss,' said Louise. 'Now you're living in a dream.'

'It's better than sexually harassing an incoming student. You know I could leak this to the press.'

'I can leak that Marcos did time in jail,' said Louise.

'You are low,' said Missy.

'All's fair,' said Louise. Louise felt powerful and invulnerable when she said this.

'You are low,' said Missy. 'But I'm lower. If you insist on taking this tack, you leave me no choice.' Missy stood, walked over to the desk and got out her phone book.

'I'm going to call him,' said Missy. 'I'm going to call him at Ricky's and tell him everything. 555-3694. I'm going to tell him the truth about Scott Feinstadt, I'm going to tell him the truth about you.'

So he *was* at Ricky's.

A mother always knows.

'What truth? What's the truth about me, Missy?' asked Louise. 'What's so fucking horrible?'

'Don't make me say it,' said Missy.

'Go on,' said Louise. 'Spit it out. There's no horrible truth about me, and you know it.'

Missy took a deep breath. She weighed the consequences. And then she went for it.

'You failed him, Louise, you know you did. You failed Scott Feinstadt and then he died.'

What was Missy talking about? She'd failed him? He'd failed her! She'd failed him?

'You know,' said Missy.

And Louise did know. The phone call. The morning that he'd left for school, the morning of his fateful ride. Scott Feinstadt had called her, Louise, and she'd failed him.

'Louise,' he'd said. She was lying on her single bed in her room in Larchmont, heartbroken and depressed and lonely. She had innocently answered the phone.

'I need to see you again before I go,' said Scott Feinstadt.

'Why?' said Louise, heart pounding now, her whole body filling with hope.

'I don't know,' said Scott Feinstadt. 'I just do.'

'Is it Missy?' asked teenaged Louise. 'Are the two of you having problems?'

'No, no,' said Scott Feinstadt. 'Missy and I are cool.'

Then what could it be? thought Louise. You just want to see one more time how much I am in love with you? You just want to go off to school, knowing I'm still available, that I'm your love slave, that you could have me when you want me? Fuck that shit, thought Louise.

'I'm busy, Scott,' said Louise, even though it was the middle of the morning and she was still in her nightgown, one of his old black concert T-shirts actually, still lying in her bed.

'I'm just feeling a little nervous now, like maybe I shouldn't be going so far away for school,' said Scott Feinstadt. And if memory served her, he *had* sounded nervous in the moment.

He'd wanted to talk. He'd wanted to talk about himself. Louise had always listened to him before. Would she listen to him now?

'This isn't a good time. Why don't you call me when you come back for the High Holy Days? I'm busy now,' Louise said.

Scott Feinstadt had sighed on the phone then. A long, audible sigh.

'OK,' he said, 'I guess. I guess it can wait till then.'

Only of course there was no then then, only of course, like with every moment in her life, there had only been a now. She'd squandered it, the now, the now she could have had with him; Louise never learned exactly what it was Scott Feinstadt had wanted to say to her. Had he wanted her to talk him out of going away? Had he wanted her to give him the confidence to go? And of course she'd confessed the whole phone call to Missy, because at the time, after his death, the fact that they hadn't talked that day, had totally, totally plagued her. It had plagued her so much, she'd done her best to forget about it all these years.

When she'd told her, when Louise had confessed the conversation to Missy, Missy had said back then, 'Maybe he knew, maybe he knew he was going to die.'

Missy had made her feel terrible.

No one was going to do that to Louise any longer.

'Fuck that shit,' said Louise, now, in the moment, at the Carlyle, now in the only moment that was the now of her life. 'Give me the phone and I'll do it myself. Better yet, give me Ricky's address and I'll do it in person.' She got up and ripped the address book out of Missy's hand.

'I'll tell him myself,' said Louise. 'I'll tell him he's come back from the dead. Fuck it, I'll tell him I failed him if you want, and I'll tell him about you, too. He'll love that, I'm sure, being told at this late date that once upon a time, he went out with you.'

'Don't,' said Missy. 'I was only grandstanding. I didn't mean it. It's a bad move; I never should have said anything, I'm telling you.'

'Like I should listen to you?' said Louise.

'I'm serious,' said Missy. 'It's a horrible strategy. You know it is. You can't tell someone they're dead. He'll go into shock or something. Give it time, we'll come up with a plan together, you and me.'

'You and me?' said Louise.

'Two heads are better, right?' said Missy. 'I've had more practice at this kind of thing, you know it's true. We'll figure it out, then we'll take him to lunch, someplace nice, we'll flatter him a little . . .'

Was she right? thought Louise. Were two heads better? Together, was there anything she and Missy couldn't do?

'Forget it,' said Louise. 'I'm telling F. Scott the truth.' And Missy's address book in hand, she walked out of Missy's suite, into the hall.

'Don't do it,' said Missy, opening the door behind her, standing in the hall in her water bra. 'Get back here.'

'No way,' said Louise.

'I'm telling you,' said Missy. 'You'll fuck it up, fuck it up like you always do. Fuck it up for everyone. Listen to me, Louise, you'll only hurt yourself.'

Louise held Missy's address book tight to her chest. She took the hotel elevator to the lobby, waved off the doorman, walked out onto Madison Avenue and hailed herself a taxi.

'Avenue D and Ninth Street,' said Louise to the taxi driver. She was alone and tough and strong. This time she was going to do what she needed to do. She wasn't going to avoid anything, this time.

<hr />

F. Scott was standing outside the tenement building when her taxi pulled to a stop. Missy must have given him the heads-up. He was standing outside waiting for her.

'Keep the change,' Louise said to the taxi driver.

She got out of the cab and closed the door. The taxi pulled away behind her.

F. Scott looked sleepy. His eyes were half-closed, his T-shirt untucked. But he was there.

'Did I wake you?' Louise asked.

'Missy woke me,' said F. Scott. 'Ricky's band is playing tonight, but I crashed early. I was tired.'

'I'm sorry,' said Louise.

'Why?' said F. Scott.

'Because, I woke you.'

'She woke me, Louise. I told you that already.'

He looked down at his feet. He was barefoot.

'You're barefoot,' said Louise.

'I know,' said F. Scott.

'Do you want to go inside?' said Louise.

'No,' said F. Scott. 'I like it out here.'

Louise looked around. The building next-door had a stoop.

'Do you want to sit on the stoop?' said Louise.

'No,' said F. Scott. 'Whatever you want to say to me, you can say it on the sidewalk.'

What did she want to say to him? What did she want to say to this sleepy kid?

'Missy said you had something really important to say to me, so go ahead, Louise. Get it over with.' He looked a little shaky when he said this, like he was angry or he was scared.

'What do you think I want to say to you?' asked Louise.

'That you want to break up?' said F. Scott. He looked like he might cry then. He shifted his weight.

'Ouch,' said F. Scott.

'What?' said Louise.

'I stepped on a piece of glass.' F. Scott inspected his foot.

'Is it cut?' said Louise. 'Is it bleeding?'

'No,' he said. 'There's just a little extra flap of skin.

'Can I see?' said Louise.

'Would you get it over with already?' F. Scott said, still trembly but with a tiny smile. 'You know, this piece of glass is a little like a shot in the foot, it will help me get over the pain in my heart.' His smile wobbled. He was trying for cavalier but he seemed sincere.

'OK,' said Louise. 'I will.'

But how? How could she possibly tell him what she didn't understand herself?

'Louise,' said F. Scott. He was losing patience.

'OK,' said Louise. 'Here's the deal. When I was a kid, when I was a kid back in high school, I had a boyfriend. I had a boyfriend who looked an awful lot like you.'

F. Scott stared at her. Then he looked at the bottom of his foot. He lifted it into a standing half-lotus, and picked at his sole.

'Go on,' said F. Scott, 'I'm listening.'

'He looked like you, he was an artist like you, I went out with him, and then, well, Missy went out with him, too.'

At this, F. Scott looked up. 'Missy?'

'Yeah. Missy. We both went out with him and then he died, he died in a car accident, if you must know . . .' and here Louise's voice gave out.

'Oh, Louise,' said F. Scott. 'That's so sad.' He moved forward to comfort her, but when he stepped on his foot, he yelped in pain.

'Can I look at that for you?' said Louise. 'Please? You don't want to get an infection.'

'It's all right,' said F. Scott. 'I'm cool.'

He held her eyes with his eyes now. Louise took a deep breath. She was powerful. Invulnerable. Strong.

'Well, he looked like you, he painted like you, he even had your name . . .'

'My name?' F. Scott interrupted her. 'You mean, F. Scott? Because the F. part is . . .'

'Scott Feinstadt. His name was Scott Feinstadt.'

'He looked a lot like me?' said F. Scott. 'His name was Scott Feinstadt?'

'His name was Scott Feinstadt and he looked exactly like you,' said Louise. 'He even had your birthday and your voice.'

Behind F. Scott was a stand of garbage pails. They were rank in the steamy heat. A rat the size of a cat jumped from one to the other. Louise gave a little start but F. Scott didn't seem to notice.

'My birthday?' said F. Scott. 'What are you saying?'

'I'm saying in almost every way you're a hell of a lot like the original,' said Louise. She felt crazy when she said this.

'The original?' said F. Scott.

'The original Scott,' said Louise.

F. Scott looked down at the sidewalk. He looked up and then down the street. He ran his palms over his buzzed head. Then he looked at her.

'You're weird, you know that?' said F. Scott.

'Yeah, I guess so,' said Louise.

'Missy thinks I'm a lot like this guy too?'

'She does,' said Louise. 'In fact, she thinks he's you. Or you're him. You know what I'm saying, don't you?'

'No one on planet Earth could know what you're saying,' said F. Scott.

'Are you him?' asked Louise. 'Are you the original Scott Feinstadt?'

F. Scott looked at Louise. She looked back at him. She was powerful, invulnerable, strong.

He wasn't.

'What do you think, Louise?'

'Hunh?' said Louise.

'You just said, Missy thinks I'm some guy back from the dead. Is that what you think?'

'Well,' said Louise. 'Yes and no.'

'Yes and no?' said F. Scott.

'Yes and no,' said Louise. 'You look like him, you sound like him, you paint like him, you kiss like him . . .'

'I kiss like him?' said F. Scott.

'You kiss like him, only better,' said Louise, telling the truth. She was into the truth now.

F. Scott stared at her.

'Did you love this guy? Did you love this guy who kissed like me?'

Louise took a deep breath. Had she loved him?

'I loved him,' said Louise.

'Oh,' said F. Scott.

It was quiet between them.

F. Scott looked down at the ground.

'Do you still love him, Louise?' asked F. Scott.

Did she? Did she still love Scott Feinstadt?

'I don't know,' said Louise.

F. Scott looked up at her. He stared at her with his cool blue eyes, the same cool blue as Scott Feinstadt's.

'What do you know?' he asked her.

What did she know? Louise answered him. 'I know I loved him with my seventeen-year-old heart, and then I know I forgot about him. I forgot about him, until you showed up.' She stopped here and thought for a moment. 'I know it wasn't finished between him and me, at least on my side. It wasn't finished when he died.'

'Not finished?' said F. Scott staring at her.

'No,' said Louise. 'He called me, he called me the day he died, he wanted to see me, but I was too hurt, I was too angry, I . . .'

'You didn't see him?'

'No,' said Louise. 'And then he died.'

The night was moist and airless. F. Scott gingerly put his injured foot down.

'And then you met me,' he said.

'Well, a couple of things happened in between,' said Louise, and she laughed a little. It felt good to get this off her chest. Was this the way Peter had felt when he'd confessed to her? 'A couple of things happened in between in the last two decades, but yes, then I met you.'

F. Scott continued staring at her.

'Why are you laughing?' he said.

'I don't know,' said Louise. 'I guess in some weird way it's all a little funny.'

'You think this is funny?' said F. Scott.

'No,' said Louise. 'Yes, a little bit. I don't know,' said Louise.

'It isn't funny, Louise,' said F. Scott. 'It isn't funny that you're in your late thirties and you're still mourning some dead punk who treated you like shit.'

Louise took a step back. So F. Scott was into the truth too.

'Well, that is true,' said Louise. 'It's not pretty, but it is true. When you put it that way . . .'

'It isn't funny that you can't get over some stupid pivotal moment from high school for God's sake that everyone else on the planet goes through, but gets over, you know, uses it to learn and gets on.'

'Well, that's true,' said Louise, thinking, how come every one else on the planet gets over these things? 'But you know, he died. Maybe if he had lived, I would have gotten over it.'

'That's where I come in, I guess,' said F. Scott. 'In your con-fused, messed-up head, I come in to help you get over it.'

'Well, yes and no,' said Louise. 'I mean, you're great,' she said, because he was great, and she was telling the truth now, wasn't she? 'And you're you . . . It's just that you look so much like him . . .'

'And I kiss so much like him,' said F. Scott bitterly.

'It's more than a passing resemblance,' said Louise. 'Missy noticed it too.'

'I think you're sick,' said F. Scott. 'I think you're both sick. In fact I think you're sick and mean.'

'I don't mean to be mean,' said Louise, all that stu-pid empowerment leaking out of her. She felt like an idiot.

F. Scott looked back at his foot again.

'I'm going back to bed,' said F. Scott.

'Now?' said Louise.

'Now,' said F. Scott.

'But I want to talk to you some more,' said Louise.

'Well, here's a news flash, Louise. I don't want to talk to you, anymore,' F. Scott said. 'I want you to go.'

'F. Scott,' said Louise. 'Wait!'

But he turned away from her and hobbled back into Ricky's building.

———

'F. Scott! I'm sorry, I just wanted to explain myself, I just wanted to talk . . .'

But F. Scott didn't want to talk to her. He closed the door to Ricky's vestibule and it locked automatically behind him.

Louise walked the eight long, lonely, scary blocks west before she could hail herself another cab. Eight blocks of wondering what she had done. Was it good to come clean? Or was F. Scott right, was she just crazy and mean? She was just crazy and mean, wasn't she? She'd fucked it up, just the way Missy had said she would. She'd been selfish and cruel. She'd acted like a boy.

The whole long night felt too horrible to contemplate, and so when Louise got home, she went straight to bed; she would figure out a way to make it up to him in the morning.

Peter was sitting on the foot of her bed when Louise woke up the next day, so early, her digital clock read 5:15. Was she still dreaming? No. It was him. How had he gotten in? For safety's sake, he'd always insisted on having a copy of her keys. He'd just never used them before.

He was sitting at the foot of her bed, fully dressed, holding his head in his hands.

'Pete,' said Louise. 'Is that you?'

Of course it was him. How many mornings had he sat this same way at the edge of their bed, for it had been their bed at one time, this same box spring and frame, this very same mattress, his head in his hands, trying to find the strength to face the day? Louise had always thought that was why Peter had his head in his hands; he was trying to find the energy to get up, to shower and shave, to take on a passel of undergraduates; it was this same lack of inspiration that had had Louise snuggling in deeper toward her pillow and feigning sleep. Never had it occurred to Louise that what Peter was actually doing was trying to find the strength to face his wife. Now, this thought made her sad. Louise sat up, drew the sheets around her, even though she was properly clothed; she was still wearing Peter's old shirt, but she felt modest, perhaps because Peter at the bed's end seemed so naked and exposed.

As she got closer Louise saw that Peter hadn't shaved, which was odd for him; Peter always shaved, shaving every day was the very definition of being Peter. He looked a little rumply, like he hadn't slept, or if he had, he'd slept in the clothes he was wearing. Louise reached out and rested a hand on Peter's shoulder.

'Peter?' she said.

'Peter?'

His shoulders began to shake, they shook beneath her hand. He was sobbing, Peter, wordlessly, Peter was sobbing, that great, big, strong and silent man.

Louise wrapped her arms around his chest to comfort him.

'Oh, honey,' said Louise. 'Don't cry.'

Saying this only seemed to make Peter cry harder.

Louise used her hands to brush away his tears, but the tears kept coming. She used her hands to stroke his cheeks, his wet and scratchy face. Peter opened his eyes; the whites were streaked with red, the blues deeper and more blue than she had ever seen them, glimmering, as they were flooded now with water.

'Don't cry, sweetie, please,' said Louise.

Peter tried to stop, he held his breath, but those sobs kept wracking through him, the tear water kept on coming. He needed to blow his nose.

'You need to blow your nose, sweetheart,' said Louise, petting his head, smoothing his hair over against his part. 'I'll get up to get you a tissue.' She moved to stand, to unwrap herself from his body and his face, from his hair and hands, for he was holding on to her now, holding on to her tentatively at first, but when she moved to get away, Peter tightened his grip; he did not want to let her go.

'Stay,' said Peter. 'Please,' he said. The tears and the sobs, they flowed through him, they flowed and flowed.

So Louise stayed. She didn't get up and get him a tissue. Instead she offered him a little corner of her sheet, and he said: 'Sure?' and Louise said: 'Sure.' Peter Harrington used the corner of the sheet to wipe his nose. Still he kept sobbing, it didn't seem that he would ever stop, until finally Louise gave in, she said: 'Cry, honey. Cry. Cry the hardest you can, cry your dearest heart out.'

Peter Harrington obeyed her. He cried his heart out in his wife's arms. He did as he was told.

———◆———

Peter must have cried them both to sleep, she had been that

exhausted, because the next thing Louise remembered was opening her eyes again several hours later and seeing Peter, not at the foot of the bed, but sharing her pillow, wrapped up in her arms. He was asleep, breathing lightly, his face washed clean of all his troubles, by his tears perhaps, or by the healing powers of sleep, even his wrinkles, his worry lines and his laugh lines, the deep etchings that framed his mouth, were gone, gone, gone; he looked like he had as a young man, when she'd first met him, when he was just a few years away from being a boy. He looked beautiful and clean and not at all fucked up, lying in Louise's arms. He looked handsome.

So although Louise had to go to the bathroom, she did not stir, she did not want to lose this moment with Peter. It was like a piece of their past had come to revisit them, like they were allowed to relive a lost and valuable moment, and because this all felt so precious, so emblematic of their early time together, Louise did not stir. Even though she really had to go to the bathroom now. She knew enough to know she might never be blessed this way again. So she held Peter in her arms and she breathed him in. For a while.

Finally, he began to wake. He rolled up enough for Louise to extricate herself and get up and go to the bathroom. She went to the bathroom and she shut the door, even though she and Peter never shut the door, they still didn't, after all those years of being married and then being not married. She shut the door, not so much to give herself privacy, but to give him privacy; she shut the door and peed, she peed and peed – all those margaritas – and as the liquid left her body she felt lighter and lighter and lighter. She felt close to happy, but something richer and more porous. At home, peeing in the bathroom, with the door closed, and her husband waking in the bedroom, she felt like a normal person.

When she wiped and flushed and washed her hands, Louise stared at herself in the mirror. Her hair was a mess, but in a good way, it had a nice tousled puff to it, and her eyes were clear. Clear-eyed Louise walked out into the bedroom. Peter was standing there, his belt open, retucking his shirt into his pants. He was pulling himself together. For her. When she entered, he looked up; he looked up and smiled. Louise smiled back. And then he zipped and rebelted, and tucked the end of his belt into his khakis. Khakis she'd helped pick out.

'Lou,' said Peter, and when he said her name, Louise realized how very little they'd spoken. They'd spoken so little these past few hours. He'd cried, they'd slept, but they hadn't spoken much at all. Still, somehow, they'd talked.

'I know,' said Louise.

She did. She knew it all, the complexity of what he was feeling, for she felt it too, in her own way, in her own conflicting way.

'I'd like to try again,' said Peter. 'I'd like to try again, with you.'

He sat down on the bed. He held out his hand to her. Louise looked at the hand closely. The very hand just days before she could not recall in her mind's eye, the hand she could not remember. It was a beautiful hand, really. Strong and stubborn and square. His nails were so rectangular they looked like little televisions. Cut neatly to the quick. Some golden hairs rode the back of his wrist and hand. She took that hand in hers and sat down next to him.

'Farrah?' said Louise.

'Yes,' said Peter. 'But she's not you.'

Louise touched his hand with her hand, she squeezed it. He was so kind to her. So generous. But did he really know her, did he know how selfish she could be? How dreadful she had been to a sweet young man the night before? Would Peter really want her if he knew her?

'I don't pretend to have a plan,' said Peter. 'I don't pretend to know what the hell I'm doing.'

'That makes two of us,' said Louise, laughing a little hoarsely. Her throat and mouth were dry.

'But I'm different than I was before,' said Peter. 'And I think you might be different too.'

Was she? Was she different than she was before? Or was she more like she was before, now, than she had been in their lousy middle? In the middle of their marriage. Or was she somebody else now, was she somebody else new now, heartless and awful and strong, most of all?

'I don't know,' said Louise.

'I know,' said Peter.

He gave her hand a squeeze.

'I trust you'll tell me when you do.'

Louise was walking Peter to the door, when the doorbell rang. Missy. Couldn't she at least have stayed away until checkout?

'Don't answer it,' whispered Louise.

'Why?' said Peter.

'It's Missy,' whispered Louise. 'She's probably come to check up on me.' To find out what went down last night, to commiserate, ultimately to gloat.

'I know, she said you had a fight, but you girls have fought before . . .' he started toward the door, but Louise stopped him.

'You talked to Missy?' asked Louise.

'She called me last night, she said you guys had had a fight, about me,' said Peter, looking a little pleased. 'She said she thought you might still be open to getting back together.'

The doorbell rang again.

'She said what?' said Louise. She hissed it. Stupid, stupid, stupid. It was stupid to think Missy wouldn't bother fighting back.

'C'mon, Louise,' said Peter. 'She was just trying to be a friend. I know she and I haven't always, but you know, she thinks we belong together. She thinks . . .'

'I can't believe her,' said Louise; she could feel her own cheeks turning red. 'That manipulative . . .'

'Relax,' said Peter. 'She means well.'

The doorbell rang again. Louder and more shrilly. Peter moved toward the door.

'Stop it, Peter,' said Louise.

'Look,' he said, 'I've got to go home and straighten up, and then I've got to get to work. By the way, I called the dean's office just in case you hadn't; I'd noticed you'd missed a day. I said you had a family emergency. I hope you don't mind; I didn't want you to get in trouble. Besides,' he said, moving an errant lock of her hair behind her ear, 'once they knew you were missing, they sounded kind of worried . . .'

Peter was still Peter.

The doorbell rang again. There was the sound of knocking.

'Please,' said Louise. 'I can't stand her.'

Peter hovered between the door and Louise.

The ringing and knocking continued.

Louise tried to hold him back.

'This is ridiculous,' said Peter. He moved forward and opened the door.

F. Scott. F. Scott Feinstadt. Standing in her hallway.

He was a mess, F. Scott. Like Peter, he hadn't bothered to shave. Like Peter, his eyes were ringed, his face was tired, his T-shirt was rumpled and stained.

'Oh, F. Scott, thank God,' said Louise.

'You,' said F. Scott, to Peter. 'I can't fucking believe it.'

'Hunh?' said Peter.

'This is why you told me all that stuff?' said F. Scott. 'Because you were going back to him? You know, Louise, most people just say something normal like, "It isn't working out" . . .'

'Excuse me?' said Peter. And then pointedly to Louise, 'Who is this?'

'An MFA applicant?' said Louise.

'An MFA applicant?' said F. Scott.

'Peter Harrington,' said Peter. He held out his hand to shake.

F. Scott did not return the gesture. F. Scott's hands hung loosely below his hips. He was still wearing the same gangbanger jeans from the night before. Louise could see his underwear, his belly and his bones.

'Peter Harrington,' said Peter. This time with a little more heft. 'Louise's husband.'

'Her ex-husband, you mean,' said F. Scott. Then, to Louise, 'Or maybe he's back from the dead too?' He was running his fingers through his buzz cut. Shifting his weight from side to side, nervously, like a boxer or a junkie.

'Excuse me?' said Peter.

'Forget it,' said Louise. She was pushing him out the door. 'Peter, you'll be late for work.'

'That's all right,' said Peter. He was squaring off his shoulders.

'No it's not,' said Louise. 'Please, Peter. I can handle this.'

Peter looked dubious. He stared F. Scott Feinstadt down. F. Scott Feinstadt stared right back at him.

'Can you?' said Peter.

'Yes,' said Louise, 'I can.' She pushed him out the door.

'I'll call you later, Lou,' said Peter.

'Fine,' said Louise.

'I'll call you in fifteen minutes,' said Peter. 'Every fifteen minutes, I'll call you.'

'OK,' said Louise. 'Call away. Have a good day, Peter. Bye-bye.'

'Good-bye,' said Peter.

'Sayonara,' said F. Scott, passing Peter by, stepping over Louise's threshold.

Peter wavered in the hallway.

'Good bye, Peter,' said Louise. Then she shut the door.

———

She and F. Scott stood in her entranceway. Silently. They listened as Peter hovered near the doorframe. They listened as they heard his footsteps hesitate down the hall. They heard the elevator door squeak open and the elevator door squeak shut. They breathed quietly together for a little while until they were convinced that he was gone.

'I don't believe you,' said F. Scott.

'What?' said Louise. 'What don't you believe?'

'You come and drop a load of shit on me and meanwhile you've got your ex-husband sleeping over. Missy warned me.'

'Missy?' Louise was incensed.

'She told me I'd find him here.'

That witch.

At first, Louise felt ashamed, ashamed and guilty and then a little bit like begging.

'It's not like that, it's not what you think . . .' He didn't understand the situation; she would make him understand.

'Peter and I are divorced,' said Louise. 'We didn't sleep together last night. The truth is, we didn't sleep together much when we got married . . .'

'I don't give a shit about him,' said F. Scott.

'Give me a chance, here,' said Louise. 'I want to explain myself. I'm sorry about what I did with you last night, it was stupid and thoughtless, it was clumsy. I don't know, I didn't know what I was doing . . . You reminded me so much of somebody, but you were different too, you were kind and fun and funny, and I was so happy being with you.' Louise surprised herself here, but it was true, being with F. Scott had been bewildering but it had made her happy. 'I guess everything I was feeling was so good but so confusing and then, you skipped out on me . . .' And when she said this, Louise realized that this was what was bothering her. 'You disappeared. You left me in bed, in bed, you left me after we slept together, without a note or a phone call . . .'

F. Scott took a step back. F. Scott got red in the face.

'I don't know,' said F. Scott. 'I know we haven't spent that much time together, I know we only slept together twice, but it just felt kind of big to me, what was going on between me and you. Too big, if you want to know the truth . . .'

Louise nodded. It had felt too big to her too.

F. Scott's hands sunk deep into his pockets. 'I woke up, and I saw you sleeping there, and you were so pretty, and so familiar and so new, and well, I couldn't stand it in the moment, you know? I needed to make sense of things, I . . . that doesn't excuse you shacking up with Wally Cleaver.'

Louise started to laugh.

'How do you know from Wally Cleaver?'

'Nick at Night,' said F. Scott. He looked like he might cry then.

'Oh, F. Scott,' said Louise. She reached out a hand, it hung in the air, but he did not come closer and neither did she, so she retracted it. 'Nothing happened,' said Louise.

'You expect me to believe that?' said F. Scott, palming his buzz cut again. 'You expect me to believe that nothing happened between you and old can't-keep-it-in-his-golf-pants over there?' He looked all jacked up on something.

'I expect you to believe me,' said Louise.

F. Scott found this last exchange hysterical. He started to laugh, he laughed and laughed; he couldn't stop laughing. He was doubled over with laughter, he found Louise's entreaty that hilarious.

'You expect me to believe you?' said F. Scott. 'What a riot.'

'What are you on?' said Louise.

'What am I on? What am I on? I must be on something, right? You tell me. You tell me what I'm on. You think I'm some idiot who came back from the dead and then you have the nerve to ask me what I'm on . . .' He shook his head, he stopped pacing. He held his head in his hands. He looked up at Louise and tears were streaming down his face.

Oh my God, thought Louise, what have I done?

'I never felt this way about anyone before, I never felt like this about anyone before you. It was like you knew me, see. It was like you knew what I was thinking, what I would say before I said it. Even with the sex . . . it was like you knew me.'

F. Scott Feinstadt was staring right into Louise's eyes, the tears streaming down his face. He wiped his nose with the back of his hand.

Louise reached out her hand, she'd wipe his nose with her own hand, she'd do that for this boy, this passionate sad and angry boy, she'd wipe his nose on her hand and then on Peter's old button-down, which she was still wearing.

F. Scott Feinstadt wouldn't let her. He waved her hand away.

'But of course you knew me, right? You knew me because I'm just some sort of a freak to you, right? The reincarnation of some guy who ditched you in high school? A doppelgänger or whatever. What did that bitch Missy call it? A fucking Frankenstein. A manifestation of all your loneliness and grief. Missy. That's the bitch who's your best friend in the world, right? You knew me, because you knew him, and me, all I am to you is some kind of a ghost freak high school ex fuck. Some visitation.'

Louise stared at F. Scott. He was wet and teary and snotty; he was melting before her eyes.

'You talked to Missy?'

'Better believe it. What else was I supposed to do?' said F. Scott. 'I was up all night. I went to every after-hours bar in the goddamn city and then I went to Missy. She told me all about you this morning. Over coffee. At her suite at the stupid Carlyle.'

Fucking Missy.

'And then,' F. Scott said, his hands were shaking. He was staring at his shaking hands. 'And then she tried to get me into bed.'

He spit on the floor. On the floor of Louise's apartment. On the wood, right next to the oriental Carpet. His little blob of spit just sat there, thick and wet and oily.

Louise didn't know what to say. Who was worse, Louise or Missy? How could they have treated F. Scott this way?

'I'm sorry, F. Scott . . . I'm . . .'

'My name isn't F. Scott,' said F. Scott. 'It's Francis. Francis Scott Key Feinstadt. My dead fucking asshole biological father was the one who named me. He was a Fitzgerald freak, all right? I used it on the application because I thought it sounded cool. Everyone at home just calls me Scotty.

'Anyway, my father didn't come from Larchmont. He came

from downtown Baltimore, and he was old enough to be my grandfather; he was my mother's literature professor, if you must know, and he was married. Feinstadt's my stepfather's name, he raised me, and he's from Cincinnati, so don't start thinking I'm your ex fuck's love child or something, Missy already tried that stuff. So unless I really am a reincarnation or some physical embodiment of the memory of somebody else . . .'

F. Scott kept shaking his head, he shook it like he was trying to shake the thoughts out.

'According to you, I'm not even an artist in my own right, I'm just some extension of his talent, some phantom limb . . .'

'That's not true,' said Louise.

'How do you know?' said F. Scott. 'You never saw my slides.'

His face was getting redder and redder. He looked like he might explode.

'Please,' Louise said. 'You'll make yourself sick.'

F. Scott grabbed his chest.

'I think I'm having a nervous breakdown.'

'Oh God, I'm so sorry, I'm sorry,' said Louise. She should have known better, she should have known that all this stuff was about her, not him, it was her baggage, not F. Scott's. She should have known F. Scott Feinstadt was bound to be a real person in the possession of a real life. She should have treated him like one. She would treat him like one now.

'I'm sorry. I'm nuts. I'm crazy. I behaved badly. I never meant to insult you . . .'

F. Scott pointed a finger in her face.

'You never even thought about me,' he said.

Louise backed up. She held up both her hands.

'Okay, Scotty,' said Louise.

'Don't call me that,' said F. Scott.

The phone rang. The answering machine picked up. It was Peter. 'Lou? It's me. If you don't pick up, I'm calling the police, I'm calling the police,' said Peter.

Louise moved to pick up the receiver. As she did, F. Scott moved toward the door.

'Don't go,' said Louise. 'Please.'

'Are you fucking kidding?' said F. Scott.

'That's it, I'm hanging up and calling,' Peter said on the phone machine.

Louise picked up the receiver.

'I'm fine, Pete, I'll call you back.' Louise hung up the phone on Peter. 'F. Scott, please don't go.'

He slammed the door. Louise went after him.

'F. Scott! Scotty, wait!' but he was already down the hall. He opened the door to the stairwell, and then F. Scott was gone, slamming the fire door behind him.

The alarm began to wail.

Inside her apartment, the phone rang again.

'Louise, it's your mother . . .'

Another call came through and cut her off. Ring. Ring. Peter. 'Louise, did you hang up of your own free will? Or did he—' Click. Missy. 'I've been trying to figure out if I should give you the heads-up or not, but the kid seemed pretty mad after I talked to hi—' Click. Ring. Ring. 'Louise? Louise? It's Mom. Is there something wrong with your—' Click. Ring. Ring.

Louise stood in her empty doorway and listened to her Mom, Peter and Missy duke it out on her answering machine. Finally she picked up.

'Missy,' she said. 'We have to talk.'

————•————

They met in the lobby of the Carlyle. Missy was sitting at a little cream-colored settee, with a pot of coffee by her elbow on a perfect little end table. The rest of the room was filled with a few well-dressed silver heads. In her Dr Blue Jeans jeans and blue V-neck cashmere sweater – it was like a meat locker in there, they'd finally gotten the AC working; so cold, Louise supposed, to help preserve all that lifted flesh – Missy looked like some out-of-place teenager; Eloise at the Carlyle; what she was, an almost-middle-aged spoiled brat. She smiled over her coffee at Louise as Louise navigated the room towards her.

'Hey, Wheezy,' said Missy. 'I dig what you did with your hair.'

Louise's hair was in a ponytail, tied up with one of Peter's old socks. For some reason, it was the first thing she had laid her hands on when, in a hurry, she'd rooted through her dresser. Instinctively, Louise reached up to feel for the sock, and then she thought, no, I'm not falling for that shit again, you can't wig me out any more, Missy, I'm immune to your crap, and so she let her hands fall back loosely towards her side.

She sat down across from Missy in an armchair.

'You were deliberately manipulative and cruel,' said Louise.

'Oh, come on,' said Missy. 'You won this round. It's not attractive to sit around and gloat.'

'Gloat?' said Louise. 'That poor boy is in agony because of us. And you said you loved him.'

'Oh, I only wanted him 'cause you had him,' said Missy. She took a sip of coffee.

Of course this was true. But still. To hear Missy admit such a thing!

'Is that true?'

'Yes, of course it's true,' said Missy. 'I mean, that's what Marcos said.'

'You told all this to Marcos?'

'Of course I did,' said Missy. She couldn't surpress her gleeful grin. 'He's taking the next plane out of Charles De Gaulle. We're going to meet in Napa for the weekend . . .'

She's a master, thought Louise. If I could only bottle some of her nerve.

It's not nerve, it's good horse sense.

'Lookit,' said Missy, 'if he were really Scott Feinstadt, well . . .' Missy let her voice trail off, and she used her hands, in lacy circles to follow after her voice, to ride her rises and swells, like an interplay of shadows on the wall. She used her hands to give her words a body. 'But this one's way too soft. The original was so much more heartless. So much sexier. Much, much more of a rogue.' She sighed here. There was grief and longing in that sigh. She missed him, too. This much was clear.

'What can you do?' said Missy. 'You can't go home again,

or whatever.' She lit up a cigarette and offered one to Louise. Louise took it. But it trembled in her hand.

Missy looked at her. There was genuine regret in Missy's expression. And affection. There was affection in Missy's expression too. The unlit cigarette was dangling from Louise's lips. Missy leaned forward and lit it for her.

'The world is random and mysterious,' said Missy. 'The biggest surprise of all, Louise, is that this time it's happened to you.'

What? What? 'What?' asked Louise.

Missy got up. 'I've got to pack, sweetchick. I don't want to miss my flight.'

'What?' said Louise. 'What's happened to me? Answer my fucking question?'

Missy picked up the check and signed it. Then she looked Louise in the eye. 'You know that old thing about snowflakes. Well maybe just this once two snowflakes came out pretty much alike, only this time you got lucky. This particular snowflake really likes you. Stranger things have happened.'

'No, they haven't,' said Louise.

'Yes, they have,' said Missy. 'Look at the history of the world.' She gave Louise an air kiss and she was gone.

Farrah was at the department's desk, the desk that was parked in front of Peter's office, when Louise arrived. Louise knew she was Farrah without the pretty young woman ever telling

Louise her name. She knew it from the silver ring that encircled her thumb, from the black nail polish peeking out of her opened-toed sandals, from the pretty black tank top and the purple batiked sarong. From the pink pashmina shawl. From the way her face fell, when she first saw Louise standing in front of her desk. It was clear Farrah knew who Louise was.

Louise was still in that same old button-down of Peter's, a pair of ill-fitting jeans that made her look hippy, and wrapped around her ponytail was that tell-tale sock.

'Is Professor Harrington in?' said Louise.

Farrah looked up. Her eyes were large and brown. She looked like a deer caught in headlights. She looked like a mugging victim when the switchblade is first sprung out. She looked up at Louise, like Louise could hurt her.

'Mrs Harrington?' asked Farrah.

'Yes,' said Louise. 'No.'

'Just Louise,' Louise said.

'I'll let him know you're here,' said Farrah.

'That won't be necessary,' said Peter. He was standing in the doorway to his office. He looked from one woman to the other. 'I was just about to take a little walk.'

'May I join you?' said Louise.

'Of course,' said Peter. 'Farrah, would you take my calls.'

Farrah looked at Peter searchingly. Her big brown eyes seemed to talk. He nodded at her, and she at him, biting her lower lip now. Louise thought she spied on Farrah's tongue the flash of a silver stud. In another world, another life, she might have fixed F. Scott up with Farrah, but not now.

'Of course, Peter . . . I mean Professor Harrington,' said
Farrah. I feel like I'm in a movie, thought Louise as she and
Peter silently walked down the hall, leaving that little girl
at that great big desk all alone. Like a murderer. Like I've
won. This wasn't just about her and Peter any more. There
were other people, now. The Harringtons were no longer two
people alone.

*You were never two people alone. There was always someone else in the
room with you.*

Thanks for reminding me.

You had your ghosts too.

Shut up, Mom.

Now, at least you've got a chance. He is your husband.

Once upon a time, Mom, thought Louise, he was.

Outside, the campus was abuzz. Frisbees flew in the breeze,
the lawn was dotted with half-clothed sunbathers. Once in a
while some student or another seemed to halfheartedly gaze
at an open book. A clothes rack full of Ecuadorian imports
was set up on the plaza, but nobody was thumbing through
the wares, and the old hippie couple who were hawking
them both sat snoozing in their respective folding chairs. At
Columbia, it was business as usual.

Still, neither Peter or Louise began to talk.

Finally, he broke the silence.

'I guess you're still alive,' said Peter.

'Yes,' said Louise. 'I am.'

'That boy scared me,' said Peter. 'You knew I was scared,
but still you didn't take my calls.'

'I told you I could handle it,' said Louise.

'So you did,' said Peter.

They continued to walk. Across campus and down the steps to Broadway.

'So, the good news, you want to hear it?' said Peter.

'Sure,' said Louise. She was in the mood to hear good news.

'Sammy's IPO was yesterday. We made a bundle, Louise, I'm telling you. Maybe not enough to retire, now. But enough to retire later. In style.' He said this proudly.

But then, 'At least, right now, we're rich on paper.'

On paper? Didn't that mean 'you never know'? And retire? Could either one of them think about retiring, now, when in some profound, deep way they both were just getting started? But why burst his bubble? In the moment, Peter was feeling good.

'Wow,' said Louise. 'So Sammy actually pulled it off.'

The world was random and mysterious.

'Did Missy have any money in it?'

'No,' said Peter, laughing. 'I don't really think so.'

Missy o. Louise 1.

Louise and Peter kept walking, each contemplating their new good fortune, wondering if it would stick.

'So now that the world's possibly your oyster, is this the part where you let me down gently?' asked Peter. There was a light teasing sound to his voice, but his eyes, when she dared to catch them, looked serious.

She smiled at him. 'Is this the part where you tell me Farrah is a real live person with a real live set of feelings?'

'She's just a kid, Louise. I mean she's helped me a lot and all, but are we going to end up together? I highly doubt it.'

Here Peter stopped; it was as if this idea had just occurred to him.

'Well, I can't say I'm surprised,' said Louise. 'I mean, it's one thing to run off with your student when you're twenty-eight, another when you're, you know, a little middle-aged.'

'You should talk,' said Peter.

Louise thought about this. She was a lot older than F. Scott, but was she too old?

'It's different, Peter,' said Louise.

'Why?' said Peter. 'Are the rules different because now they apply to you?'

Well, yes, thought Louise. Maybe the rules were different when she had to apply them to her one big chance at life. Maybe the rules were different when they were wrong. Maybe there were no rules when you finally found someone you could love.

They continued to walk. She remembered Farrah's eyes now. She remembered how round they had been when Farrah had looked at her. Was that the shape Louise's own eyes had been when she'd seen Scott Feinstadt and Missy together so long ago? Was that the size and shape F. Scott Feinstadt's had been when she and Missy told him their long sordid stories? When he found Peter alone with her in her apartment? Was that the size and shape her own eyes were when F. Scott Feinstadt had walked out her door?

'Look,' said Peter, 'do I have to say it, or do you?'

'It's not going to work between us,' said Louise. 'Even though we love each other.'

'No,' said Peter, 'it's not going to work between us.' He

smiled sideways at her. 'Even though we love each other.' And then he took her hand in his.

She walked him slowly back to his office.

F. Scott was sitting on the marble floor outside Louise's office when Louise finally remembered she had a job. She'd taken the long route, leaving the physics building and heading out to Broadway, stopping for a falafel and a soda, then a short walk to the park and the river, where she spent a long time looking at the current, thinking about what it might feel like to dive into that murky fast-moving water and try to swim. Then she'd walked back to campus.

He was sitting on the floor in front of her office, drinking a cup of coffee out of a paper bag.

'F. Scott,' she said.

'Louise,' he said. He handed her an envelope. A Dear John letter?

'From you?' said Louise. 'To me?'

'Nah,' said F. Scott. 'It was taped to your door.'

Louise slowly ripped open the envelope. She scanned the first few lines: 'Congratulations! You have now been appointed the permanent Admissions Coordinator for Columbia University's School of the Arts . . .'

Louise felt like laughing out loud. Instead, she turned to F. Scott.

'I'm sorry,' said Louise. 'I'm sorry about all of it.'

'You are?' said F. Scott, with surprise in his voice. 'You are, Louise? Not me.'

Louise sat down next to him. The marble of the hallway floor felt cool even through the seat of her jeans. He was a beautiful boy. But not really a boy any more, not really. There were some preliminary lines on his face, etching out his future, telling her what his future just might look like; kind, intelligent, troubled, serious, more complex than he had initially seemed; what his future just might turn out to be. With Scott Feinstadt there had been no knowing the man to come, even though she had tried to picture this at night when he was sleeping, when she had gazed with love upon his sleeping face when his parents had gone away for the weekend, or even when he was sleeping with Missy, when she was alone at night, alone in the dead of night, in the dead of night near morning, Louise could still count on his eyes being closed, she could still count on his even breathing, the little open puddle of his mouth, the little silvery dab of spit on his pillow; she'd wait and wait for the middle of the night because then she could picture him sleeping and it didn't matter who he was sleeping next to. Scott Feinstadt was alone in the bubble of his slumber. Which was why his death had proven to be such a comfort to her; in death he was alone, maybe not with her, but not with anyone else not-her. In death alone Louise had won, but now with F. Scott, F. Scott who was not dead, F. Scott who was not sleeping, the man to come and the boy he'd been, were sitting there together on the university steps beside her, doubly exposed, one self layered upon the other. For all that he resembled Scott Feinstadt, he'd behaved entirely differently. He possessed a beating heart.

'I'm not sorry,' said F. Scott. 'Because now I've met you. And if I didn't come to you from another life, maybe you would never have picked me up like you did, and then I would never have had the chance to know you. Which was kind of nice, knowing you, that is until you sort of tore my fucking guts out, I mean.'

He was smiling at her, but he looked miserable. He looked like he wanted to ask her a question, but he didn't dare to speak.

Louise decided to answer it for him. 'You're not from another life,' said Louise. 'You're from this one.'

'Well, that's good to know,' said F. Scott, markedly relieved. 'So you don't really think I'm dead or anything . . .'

'No,' said Louise. 'Scott Feinstadt is dead.'

He was dead. Scott Feinstadt was dead. She'd loved him and he was dead. Maybe if he wasn't dead, she wouldn't have kept on loving him. But he was dead, and she'd kept on loving him, whether she was aware of it or not, whether he'd deserved it or not. And he hadn't even wanted it, her love, all that eternal love and he'd squandered it. Scott Feinstadt was dead. So big fucking deal.

He was dead as a doornail. He was over. No postscript to this letter.

'He's dead, and you're not him,' Louise said.

It took a moment for the enormity of this line to sink in. If F. Scott was not an avatar of Scott, than he was something real. Maybe what Missy said was true, the world was random and mysterious. Maybe this was Louise's chance. Her one chance at a real and lasting love . . . This scared her.

Her heart, that faltering muscle, that generator of panic

and fear, it skipped a beat, and all of a sudden she couldn't breathe. Really. Louise Harrington couldn't breathe, try as she might, her heart beating wildly, as if it were sprouting wings and trying to lift itself out of her chest, chasing all the air out of her lungs until they were flat and empty. She was gasping and gasping and turning red, reaching for air, with her internal arms, desperate now for oxygen. 'I can't breathe,' gasped Louise. 'Really.' As if anyone with eyes could have possibly doubted her.

Without air, the world turned as brown as the brown paper of his paper bag, and what she could still see, even as she was suffocating, was brown and white and spotty, but it looked a lot like F. Scott Feinstadt. It looked a lot like F. Scott Feinstadt looking awfully concerned. Like he believed her. Like he knew that she wasn't faking. Like he knew she couldn't breathe. She was going to faint. Louise thought, I'm going to pass out now. I'm going to pass out now or I'm going to die. The last thing I'll ever see is F. Scott believing me.

No such luck. You'll live on to see a lot of things.

'Here,' said F. Scott. He took his cup of coffee out of the bag and put the bag over her mouth and nose. He held the bag nice and steady. He held the bag with one hand and with the other he pet her hair. 'Here,' he said, 'breathe deep.'

What would Scott Feinstadt have done in this situation? Louise didn't know, and she didn't care. Instead, she listened to F. Scott.

She breathed. Louise Harrington breathed deeply into that brown paper bag. She breathed and breathed, and surprisingly, the color came back into the world, into the world and into her cheeks.

'Breathe, Louise,' F. Scott said. His voice was full of care and concern. It was full of comfort.

Louise listened to him. She concentrated. She breathed. And then, remarkably, her breath became automatic, it took on a life of its own. Once again, Louise breathed without having to think. The brown paper bag fluttered from her hands onto the marble floor.

With her mind free now, she could focus it on other things. Like F. Scott. He was looking at her with wonder. God, he was great. Like she was his reason for being. She felt an overwhelming surge of love for him.

'F. Scott?' said Louise.

He looked down at the brown paper bag. He reached over and retrieved it. For a moment, he held it in his hands. When she thought she couldn't stand it, when she thought she couldn't stand his not-looking at her for another moment, F. Scott looked up at Louise, and her heart lifted. He looked up at her and gave that brown bag a little triumphant wave in the air. She smiled at him. He cracked his terrific grin, a grin so full and generous and happy, Louise couldn't help but laugh right back at him. He looked like a man in love. How did she get so lucky?

'Wow,' said Louise. 'It works.'

Helen Schulman is the author of the short story collection *Not A Free Show*, and the novels *Out Of Time* and *The Revisionist*. She is co-editor, along with Jill Bialosky, of the essay anthology *Wanting a Child*. Her non-fiction and fiction have appeared in such places as *TIME*, *Vanity Fair*, *GQ*, *Vogue*, *The New York Times Book Review*, *The New York Times Style Section*, *BookForum*, *The VLS*, *The Paris Review*, and *Ploughshares*, among others. She has been a Sundance Fellow, a New York Foundation for the Arts recipient and a Pushcart Prize winner. She has written several screenplays, and has taught most recently in the MFA program at Columbia University and at the Bread Loaf Writers' Conference.

A NOTE ON THE TYPE

The text of this book is set in Linotype Sabon, named after
the type founder, Jacques Sabon. It was designed by Jan
Tschichold and jointly developed by Linotype, Monotype
and Stempel, in response to a need for a typeface available
in identical form for mechanical hot metal composition and
hand composition using foundry type.

Tschichold based his design for Sabon roman on a fount
engraved by Garamond, and Sabon italic in a fount by
Granjon. It was first used in 1966 and has proved an
enduring modern classic.